THE AFTER DINNER GAME

Malcolm Bradbury is one of the sharpest and most penetrating social satirists writing in Britain today. Critically acclaimed and devotedly read, his bestselling books include EATING PEOPLE IS WRONG, STEPPING WESTWARD, WHO DO YOU THINK YOU ARE? (a collection of short stories) and THE HISTORY MAN, all of which are available in Arrow. THE HISTORY MAN was, of course, dramatized in a highly acclaimed BBC television series in 1981.

Malcolm Bradbury is currently Professor of American Studies at the University of East Anglia.

MALCOLM BRADBURY
THE AFTER DINNER GAME
Three plays for television

ARROW BOOKS

Arrow Books Limited
17–21 Conway Street, London W1P 6JD

An imprint of the Hutchinson Publishing Group

London Melbourne Sydney Auckland
Johannesburg and agencies
throughout the world

First published in 1982

Set in AM Compset Bembo by
Photobooks (Bristol) Limited
Barton Manor, St Philips, Bristol

Made and printed in Great Britain by
The Anchor Press Ltd, Tiptree, Essex

ISBN 0 09 927910 X

To
Rob Knights

CONTENTS

Introduction

Every novelist who ventures out of his or her conventional patch of fiction-writing into the world of television drama probably does this in a spirit of anxiety and terror. After all, novels are what you think you know how to write, what you have become professional in, what you have learned to express your strongest artistic desires in; television is a strange world into which you are an innocent intruder. Writing fiction, if you are serious about it, is a difficult art, but it is also a fascinatingly private one. Rather like marriage as it used to be, it takes the form of a lasting and intense relationship conducted with a sole partner: there is the novelist and the form, the necessary form of this particular book. Rather like marriage as it is now, this intense relationship can last for anything up to five or ten years – and in my own case usually the latter, because I am that kind of novelist who hates to let go of a book. A book is enormously nice to live with. Deep intimacies are contracted, the most intense frankness may be achieved; the exact tone and feel of the relationship, the ultimate style of it all, is pursued with great care and scruple. The intimacy must be exact: the pacing, the spacing, the delays and the outcomes. The outside world is the intruder, until the moment comes when it is clear that the relationship is peaked and to continue would be destructive. Severance ensues: the book is typed up in a form as final as it can be, is exposed to others, put into print. And then the void left has to be filled with a new book, which begins at first as a stranger, an oddity, until once again intimacy evolves, and one discovers once more that – apart perhaps from a dog – there is nothing like a novel for lasting companionship.

So it is with a novel; but writing a television play is nothing like this at all. Television plays have certain resemblances to novels and are often, indeed, made out of them, sometimes to their improvement. They have parallel elements: stories and plots, complications and diversions, beginnings and middles and, if they are old-fashioned, ends as well. Therefore anyone who writes a novel ought likewise to be able to write a television play. Of course there are technicalities to learn, and the pace of creation is notably faster and much more under the control of others, for television is notoriously a matter of diaries, dates and deadlines. Yet in Britain we still make a virtue of the single play on television, and we have something like a writers' theatre – in the sense that a serious work will be seriously made by directors of a high standard and with able and notable casts, and the writer's work will be granted a reasonable measure of respect and a separate independence. A significant number of our best writers have now developed primarily through the medium, and it has come to seem part of the necessary repertoire of the genres. It hence offers many a temptation to the innocent novelist, who might be inclined to suppose that you can step from the one medium to the other with a minimum of re-training. In fact this is far from true. The step is enormous and the change of situation profound. And it is not just that television has a different grammar, and means learning a radically new set of codes. It is also that television is a radically different kind of institution, and takes a very different view of the writer and the work. It is true that a novel, when finished, enters the world of the media, an ambiguous and suspect modern world; but, in my own case at least, it does not start there and does not end there. Television, however, is that world institutionalized; and a television play enters it from the very moment of conception.

Yes, it is true that the single play is a cornerstone of the British television system, but it remains an eccentric and somewhat isolated element. What is more, it is the single play caught up in and conditioned by television's endless running serial, that unceasing flickering gush of images and forms that is always fighting the fearful blankness of the screen; it hence becomes one fleeting episode in that depressing, tireless and open-ended visual narrative that we have more or less come to think of as modern life itself. To create that endless series, there are massive organizations which, like all modern institutions, function not only primarily through but also *for* the large hierarchies and the large office buildings which are the plant behind the screen. Television is a series run for its cautious executives, its programme-planners, its lifts and studio facilities, its dining rooms and auditors. Creativity, like a Hockney in the boardroom, is part of the purchased decor. Writing television plays is a way of entering a world of long corridors and ringing telephones; the institution is present from the start. Before the play begins to exist as a script, it has to be operated as an idea – an idea which is taken up, compared with many another idea, filtered through many minds, some creative and some not, and digested by a corporate system. If the machine says proceed, then, under pressure, a script begins to emerge, but it is not a script like the typescript of a novel. Rather what is being constructed is a set of instructions or an advisory manual for the generating of a large, expensive collective enterprise. Producers, watching money, will consider it, asking whether the French Revolution is absolutely necessary, or whether it can just be referred to in dialogue. Directors will examine it, to see whether it fits in with their style and creative intentions. The text will be rightly sifted for its cost, its length, its relevance, its effectiveness. Decisions will be taken about whether it should be filmed or videotaped, made in studio or on location, shown to children or adults, to the general audience or some specialist coterie watching in the remote hours on the lesser channels. Then the text has to be re-written and re-written again; indeed a television play is never really written at all, it is only re-written. The play you see is the sum of its re-writes.

Thus, where novels are fictions that exist between two imaginations, that of the writer and that of the reader, the television play activates an enormous actuality. Directors say good-bye to their children and block out months in their diaries. Actors appear to do a readthrough and so to commit themselves to roles and impersonations that will keep them standing cold on street corners or huddled in bleak church halls for an extended period of their lives. Set designers now begin

11

building the houses of their dreams, grander by far than anything you had written. Exotic costumery is rented or purchased; cameramen look up airline timetables and remember the addresses of small hotels in the country. Planes are chartered, houses hired and then totally refurnished to make them into something quite different, streets in the centres of great cities are blocked off, caterers with steaks assemble, men with booms chat up girls with makeup, Ford Cortinas tote tons'-worth of film-stock, and always on the edge of it all stand girls in kneewarmers holding clipboards, their function never entirely clear. Around all this, in a state of semi-mystification, half-needed and half-redundant, the writer slinks, the writer who with the words on paper he has written has set all this totally unlikely machinery into operation – these charabancs and trucks, this moving army, these actorly upsets, these late-night affairs in Birmingham hotels, these headaches, these tandoori meals at one in the morning, these blondes and redheads, these cutaways, two-shots and noddies, these crises as time runs out with nothing in the can, these people waiting, waiting and waiting, with such striking good humour and such unprotesting malleability, until one comes to believe that it is for this endless mobile party, this dreamer's holiday, that it has all been written in the first place.

And then suddenly the actors have gone, turned into something else, the Cortinas have moved elsewhere, the sets dismantled, the streets returned to their conventional users, the cameraman remembers a wife; and the object becomes object again, reel after reel of moving holiday prints, waiting to be edited, re-ordered, rough-cut and re-composed. Actors turn into images once more; the play becomes closer to what it was in the study, yet also an object entirely different, the work of innumerable hands. Then, one night, lateish, when most people are out anyway, the whole massive and costly enterprise comes to its ostensible climax – which is not really its real climax at all, but a curious sad afterbirth. It is *shown*, normally up against 'The Two Ronnies', 'Match of the Day' or something else of far more compelling interest on the other channels. Everyone involved in it waits: a serious reviewer or two notices, normally comparing it with the rest of that week's unending series of television experiences, the new programme on underwater snooker, the latest attempt at a cultural series with David Hockney in it, the newest spectacular with some fresh ego explicating the cosmos. Friends are nice, and the telephone is liable to ring several times; there will be talk, usually frustrated, of a repeat. But usually the film goes into a vault or the scrapyard, the mild discussion stops, the void closes in, the endless babble of cultural chat turns to other things; and the writer goes back into his study, that place of safe words and quiet thoughts, wondering whether anything except an unremarkable tandoori dinner or two did actually happen to anybody at all.

So you will see that writing television plays is really a very long way away from writing novels, where none of these sorts of thing happen at all, and the invented world stays within the reasonable comfort of one's own head; and they are actually a kind of opposite, a strange way of stepping out from the imagined into what some people might mistakenly call the real world. Television plays are an activation of many types of offscreen and onscreen human behaviour, generating a complex pattern of enacted images, shaped both by the social and the ever-increasing technical sophistication of those images. Writing a television play is an act of profound self-instruction in the grammar of inventive writing itself, a process in which one is simultaneously trying to guide and shape the massive fleshing out of the imaginative drives that set writers to work in the first place, and testing out the possibilities of narrative sequence and development, the growth of image and sign, in a collective situation with developing collective laws. This requires a slow learning process, and what one learns inevitably has a shaping effect on one's very ideas of writing itself – so that, since I started writing plays for television, I have found my thinking about the novel changing considerably. To date I have written seven television plays, of which five have been made and shown, one never made, and one three times started on its way and never completed, though it is the one I like best. This book unstores, in their writing order, three of those plays from their condition of post-production silence. I am very glad to have them on display as scripts, partly because they all have some relation to the novels and stories I have written, and partly because they are different plays with different ideas not only of subject but of the medium, and to me at least they show my changing ideas of image-narrative and my learning process. That sort of learning a writer conducts best if he has good directors to work with, and I have been very lucky in the two who directed these plays: Rob Knights, from whom I learned enormously, and Michael Heffernan, who, with different expectations, opened several fresh doors.

And so to the plays. The first of these, 'The After Dinner Game', was shown in 1975 and came about because David Rose, the producer, and William Smethurst, his script-editor at BBC Birmingham, wanted for the 'Play for Today' series a play set in a new university. Birmingham under David Rose has been a notable centre of serious drama, and the thought was exciting. At the time I was approached I was just finishing my novel *The History Man*, and the ending of that book was plunging me in gloom; I felt like moving into a less private, more collaborative medium. And there was another reason for seizing the opportunity. *The History Man* left me with a kind of guilt about my treatment of the subject. It was a book about the way the traditional humanism of the universities had been, over the turn into the 1970s, attacked from within by a new post-humanist radicalism. What it didn't tell was another story: the way that humanism was also being threatened from without, by something we are all now very familiar with, the new sado-monetarism. Economic functionalism has proved in the event to be a threat far greater to the universities than was the radical utopianism of the affluent early 1970s. And, since the fate of humanism is, I suppose, the abiding theme behind my writing, I wanted to venture on a second story. The risk of taking it on was that the play would steal away material from, or otherwise interfere with, *The History Man*; I wanted it to be a companion piece, but different. One way of making it different was to write it with someone else, and so I drew in a university colleague and close friend, Christopher Bigsby, with whom I'd enjoyed writing revue. Inevitably the style of the play was collaborative, too, somewhere between my work and his; and the new university we constructed was a very different establishment from the University of Watermouth in *The History Man*. It was not one of the new universities founded amid the educational excitements and the relative affluence of the early 1960s, but a fictional new university just coming into existence in the mid-seventies, when times were harder, and the problems of relating humanistic intentions to economic realities and new cries of educational relevance were much greater.

The rules were clear. It was to be a studio play, on video-tape with just a little film, a fairly small cast, and a concentrated set. As a 'Play for Today' a degree of naturalism and topicality was called for, but we fought for it to be a comedy. The play's relevance now looks even sharper when the universities are actually now facing on a very large scale the kind of cuts that the play's vice-chancellor is worrying about; but the knife was already being sharpened when we were writing. So the aim was a comedy about the conflict between humane values and a rigorous economic relevance; to reconcile the two we would need a vice-chancellor of a certain Machiavellian cunning, a man of plots. (I happen to be obsessed, as a novelist should be, by plots and plotters, the story-makers of the world.) So Bartley Humbolt came into existence. To provide the contending faculty, I imported from the University of Watermouth a secret favourite character of my own, the social psychologist Flora Beniform; Chris Bigsby introduced Patterson, the baby-dominated token underling who is put on all the committees to placate the younger faculty, because he appears to be the least troublesome of them all. (He has extended this role in a recent radio series Chris Bigsby and I went on to write.) For me, the play has very much the feel of a first play, and its studio production meant that it had to be a play more of words than images, of verbal and emotional conflicts held in one place and around one table rather than spreading through space and time. But, excellently directed, it proved the fascination of television grammar, the obsessive power of the studio and its images; and so, with the same producer and director, I went on to write a second play.

This went through various titles; my preferred one was

'The First Cod War', but it emerged, when it was shown in 1977, also in the 'Play for Today' series, as 'Love on a Gunboat'. This time the rules were more open: there was the possibility of more film, a larger cast, and a fuller use of the mechanisms of television, particularly as regards flashback. So the theme began to develop around an essential contrast that fascinated me: the spirit of youthful existence in the tight, unaffluent and moral world of the 1950s and the mood of the more affluent, more political and more historically uncertain 1970s, when those moral youths were entering an anxious and self-critical middle age. It was to be about my feeling that moral convictions had been displaced by a sense of style, and that this had led to a division between a view of oneself as a moral performer and one's more ironic sense of oneself as an absurd actor in society's contemporary, fashion-conscious dance. The mood was to be that of sad comedy, the theme the way we lead life in our kind of history, somewhere between its public motion and its contemporary ideas of self-realization, and the private spaces where we feel a consequential moral emptiness. So it was to be a play of two time-structures: it was to open up, with a question mark, that twenty-year space between 1956, the year of Suez and Hungary, and 1976, when British imperial skirmishings were reduced to a small Cod War with Iceland, and the ego-revolution was in full swing. One of the excitements of television is that a sophisticated grammar of quick cutting and time-change has established itself as a commonplace (in fiction it is still often thought of as 'experimental'). And so for me it was a step towards the freedoms that television construction offered, as well as being a means for telling a story that obsesses me: the revolt from a stable moral perception of the world into the uneasy politics of style and generations.

Perhaps I should explain that I belong myself to a generation fascinated by the year 1956 – the year in which I returned from a liberating intellectual voyage to the United States, where I had been teaching punctuation and underlining and the comma amid the cornfields at a Middle Western university, to an England that seemed, still, to be stuffy and dense, like a tea-cake, yet undergoing a crisis of national self-doubt and stepping very dangerously to the brink of war. It was the mid-fifties England of the New Elizabethans, as the fashionable phrase had it: austerity seemed over at last, the spirit of postwar materialism was just beginning to take off, and you could get Dundee cake, chocolate off ration and washing machines at last. You could also go into that daring continental innovation, the espresso bar, order a cup of froth, and immediately find a crowd of your peers – the new welfare state young, the lower middle-class or working-class young men who had been pushed upward by the Butler Education Act, done grammar school and university, and were now all writing theses or novels. Already these were fictional characters in the new novels of Anger, and the dominant play of the year was indeed John Osborne's 'Look Back in Anger', which gave this generation its stage voice. Generational feelings were strong among the young, as the imperial illusion began to crumble around the events of Suez and the Russian tanks went into Hungary to crush the liberal revolt there. 1956 was the year that made the fifties *feel* like the fifties, and the young feel that they had a difficult new world to make.

It was a gloomy time, a time of existentialism and solemn moral anxieties – moral solemnity being to the Serious Fifties what sex, politics and liberation came to be for the Swinging Sixties, and economic crisis for the Sagging Seventies. The gathering young were, for reasons not quite clear to me, mostly northern, from Leeds, Wakefield or Nottingham, where I lived; and you talked about Jean Paul Sartre, the Bomb, D. H. Lawrence, F. R. Leavis, and Maturity. Your intention was to become life-enhancing, which meant being an existential outsider (like Colin Wilson, then reading Nietzsche, according to the press, in a sleeping bag on Hampstead Heath) but also seeking mature and felt relationships. Sex being then in very short supply – most of it was rationed and exported to the troops in Germany – this meant that Maturity was eventually getting married and taking work; but a new kind of marriage, a new kind of work, a new kind of being. And all this was the dream of the fifties, which I have tried to catch in the comedy of the play; a dream that qualified and changed as the year went on, the troops went into Suez, the Hungarian refugees appeared in Britain, the garden of Eden failed, the dream of a new moral empire itself started to look as doubtful as the old empire of power began to crumble, moral issues turned into ideological issues, and the way to the national unease, the vague and never quite understood disenchantments, the guilty affluence, the unsatisfied middle-aged self-distrusts, all began, to feed the unstable seventies and, I hope, the mood and rationale of the play.

And that is the link between it and the third play here, 'Standing in for Henry', which was shown in the 'Playhouse' series in 1980. In the interval I had written another play, 'See A Friend This Weekend', never made, where I tried to move from extensive narrative and naturalism toward a more mannered and formal economy; naturalism seems to me to have exhausted itself as a television cliché, representing an enormous over exertion of the subject at the expense of the manner, and it is time for us to question its conventions of referentiality. 'Standing in for Henry' was commissioned by a new television director, Michael Heffernan; it had to be made in a hurry, with a small budget, small set and small cast. The limitations were tight, but they gave me the chance to try to write a play which had an exact tone and a strong image: that image was for me the image of a sensuous face moving amid drink, music and art, a face representing a dream of success that was half aesthetic and half corrupt, that was stylish and decadent, transforming yet already nearly betrayed – an image that seems to me to pass through much of the art and the style, the fashion and the music of the later 1960s and early 1970s. So the play was to fill the space between 1956 and 1976, and to try to catch the point at which the dream of stylish success was still hovering on the edge of innocence. The right setting therefore seemed to be a provincial advertising agency, just trying to fantasize itself towards modern success; the right central character seemed to be a young man just leaving school and hoping to succeed in the artistic world who finds that in a world of role hunger even innocence is a role. A play about the dreaming fictions out of which our sense of style and society is made up, it comes closer to my present notion of television drama as a form for exploring not so much the naturalistic face of society but of the modes by which we fictionalize it and ourselves into existence.

For the danger of television is that it is a medium which allows its own habits to become rules, its own technology to be the only real means of generating artistic change. Its possibilities in drama lie in penetrating the nature and the ambiguity of its own signs, which is what some of its best playwrights (like David Hare, Stephen Poliakoff and Ian McEwan) constantly do. At its best television drama can haunt, disturb, estrange and parody the familiar and often facile images it so readily and frequently constructs. At the moment that is its interest for me, an interest that makes me feel that it is as important in my writing life as the novel form itself.

Malcolm Bradbury
September 1981

THE AFTER DINNER GAME

The After Dinner Game was shown in the BBC-1
'Play for Today' series on 16 January 1975, with the
following cast:

Professor Mark Childers	Timothy West
Helen Childers	Georgine Anderson
Bartley Humbolt	Rupert Davies
Gaynor Humbolt	Margaret Whiting
Ben Good	Mark Wing Davey
Lee-Ann Good	Connie Booth
Andrew Patterson	Ian Gelder
Flora Beniform	Diane Fletcher
Mason, The Steward	Ronald Mayer
Waitress	Marguerite Young

Script Editor	William Smethurst
Designer	Ian Ashurst
Producer	David Rose
Director	Robert Knights

1 The vice-chancellor's office

It is an opulent high-rise office which overlooks the campus of a new – a very new – university. At the window stands the vice-chancellor, **Bartley Humbolt***, looking down from on high over his creation. We can see that the architect has had a very modern vision: we see glass walls, high towers, shuttered concrete, the steel frames of buildings in the process of construction. Down below among the buildings, people pass, small figures. Most of them are students coming in to their classes. These are eighteen-year-olds in mildly exaggerated clothing – long skirts, wide hats, patched jeans. Over this scene, we hear modern commercial music – perhaps containing an echo of the Cadbury's chocolate jingle, about the pace of life in the seventies.*

2 The university campus

From Humbolt's office the camera zooms slowly in to pick up **Mark Childers** *as he comes on to the campus. He is the Professor of History, about forty, sensitive face, in a duffel coat, carrying an old briefcase. He is the typical shabby don. A striking contrast with the students and the inhuman high buildings. We follow him inside, into the main university building.*

After we identify him, we hear **Childers'** *and* **Flora'***s first speeches.*

Flora: Mark, you bloody liberal. That polite humane intelligence of yours isn't much use now, you know.

Childers: Oh, come. He may not be such an unmitigated disaster.

3 The senior common room

The 'clunk' of a coffee machine. A shot of the machine dispensing coffee into a plastic cup. **Childers** *takes the cup, and the shot widens to show* **Flora** *and* **Childers** *together drinking beside the machine.* **Flora Beniform** *is between thirty and forty, a big woman, attractive and intelligent: a senior lecturer in social psychology. She is, however, one of those people who have mortgaged their intellect to a single orthodoxy, which they strive to serve*

despite their own sense of vital individuality. Her response to
Childers *is one of impatience, but also a real respect.*

Childers: I doubt if half the things I've heard about
him are true.

Flora: They're true. Christ, Mark, don't you know the
enemy when you see him? To Mr Good, this
university is just . . . one big intellectual Sains-
bury's.

Childers: There's no sugar in this. It's just hot water
and lumps of coffee powder. Is yours all right?

Flora: Yes, Mark. Now concentrate the mind. What
are you going to *do* about him?

Childers: I didn't know you'd even met him.

Flora: I haven't. What's that got to do with it?

Childers: He may be all right. I've met him. He stood
next to me in the urinals at the faculty lavatory.

Flora: Fascinating. I thought he just had a service
every five thousand miles.

4 The university campus

The conversation between **Childers** *and* **Flora** *continues in
sound. In vision, we see* **Ben Good** *coming into the university.
He is the new professor of organizational sciences, en route for his
inaugural lecture. He is thirty-two, burly, good looking. He wears
a dark business suit and carries a smart black documents case, with
airline labels. He smokes a panatella cigar. A swinging, arrogant
air: he is at home in this or any environment: the don as young
executive.*

Childers: Well: I must go and robe for his inaugural
lecture.

Flora: You're going?

Childers: I'm in the platform party.

Flora: The vice-chancellor trying to keep you sweet.
Refuse.

Childers: No, Flora. Just because I'm opposed to him

in principle doesn't mean I have to be ill-mannered.

Flora: That's what your epitaph will be: civil to the last.

Childers: The trouble with you Marxists is that you're modern Calvinists: all sheep and goats.

Flora: Whereas to you liberals, of course, goats are just sheep from broken homes. Well, you'll learn, Mark. He'll finish you, unless you fight. Which I hope you do, and not let yourself be conned by our illustrious vice-chancellor.

5 A corridor, outside a paternoster (*moving compartments serving as lift*)

Humbolt, **Childers** and **Good** *meet, shake hands, and one by one get into the paternoster lift.*

6 Inside the paternoster

Titles over stylized shots of **Childers**, **Humbolt**, **Good** *descending in the separate compartments of the paternoster.* **Childers** *and* **Humbolt** *are in their academic regalia:* **Humbolt** *in modern robes,* **Childers** *in shabby Oxford ones.* **Good** *remains in his business suit, and still carries his documents case.*

7 A large lecture hall

An audience awaits the arrival of the platform party. In the front row, we see **Gaynor Humbolt** *and* **Helen Childers**. **Gaynor**, *the vice-chancellor's wife, a dramatic, dressy woman in her forties, is just arriving.* **Helen**, *Mark Childers' wife, is seated. She is by contrast undramatic: pleasant-looking but rather plainly dressed, blue-stocking style.*

Gaynor: Helen, my dear. I can't get over it. Everybody looks so *clean*.

Helen: They've had the vacation to wash in.

In the second row, gowned figures: the faculty. The camera picks out **Flora Beniform** *and* **Andrew Patterson**, *sitting together.* **Patterson** *is a rather uncoordinated young man in his late twenties.*

Flora: How's the menage, Andrew?

Patterson: Fine. Everyone else says, 'How's the family?' Only you say, 'How's the menage?'

Flora: That's the difference between a citizen and a sociologist.

Now the platform party proceeds down the centre aisle. In addition to **Humbolt**, **Childers** *and* **Good**, *there is the* **registrar**. *He is also robed, leaving* **Good** *conspicuously unrobed. The procession is impressive and* **Good** *stands out. Heads turn.*

Patterson: Doesn't he have a gown?

Flora: Battersea Tech. They just award them clean overalls on graduation.

The party mounts the rostrum.

Helen: [*Solemnly*] I've got this terribly intelligent prisoner in my class who's writing a thesis on Shelley. I believe he raped someone. But the governor's being awfully decent. He's letting him have all the books and everything.

Gaynor: Oh, really? I suppose it's preferable to be raped by someone who knows an iambic pentameter when he sees one. [*Watching* **Good**] Do you find him attractive?

Helen: My rapist?

Gaynor: No, our new professor: The whizz-kid. The man with the money.

Helen: [*Looking*] Passable, I suppose.

Gaynor: Well, he's not going to jump out of a helicopter just to give you a box of chocolates, but I think he's rather sweet.

The platform party sits in noble chairs on the stage.

Flora: He's vile, isn't he? Would you buy a used car from him?

Patterson: You're a snob, Flora. Have a toffee.

Humbolt *rises from his chair and proceeds to a lectern on the other side of the stage. There is a similar lectern for* **Good**. *Slight restiveness in the audience.*

Humbolt: This is a new university, a four-year-old university, and as yet a small one. We have few traditional occasions. But today it is my pleasure as vice-chancellor to preside over what in older universities is a familiar event – an inaugural lecture by a new professor. Professor Good has come to occupy our new chair of Organizational Studies. Now what, many of my colleagues are asking, is that? [*Shot of* **Childers**' *face: he is impassive. Shot of* **Flora**'s: *she is contemptuous.*] Well, we shall hear in a moment. But here a new professor means a new subject, a new stage of growth, a new social purpose. This is why I take great pleasure in introducing Professor Good. Professor Good has had a varied career. At MIT, in the States. At Bradford, where he initiated a whole new era of industrial consultancy. [**Flora** *pulls a face.*] In industry itself, with some of our greatest corporations. And now here, where he will begin an entirely new school of studies. Professor Good.

Good *rises and goes to the lectern. Applause. We glimpse* **Flora** *who is studiously not applauding.* **Humbolt** *faces* **Good** *and doffs his academic cap.* **Good**, *with a faint parody, faces* **Humbolt** *and mock-doffs the cap he is not wearing. Renewed applause and cheers from students at the back.* **Good** *opens the folder in front of him.* **Humbolt** *goes and sits down.*

Good: Mr Vice-Chancellor, ladies and gentlemen. We live in crisis times. Crisis times for universities, as for everyone else. I'm afraid that we have clung rather too long to an outdated notion of the university: an ivory tower of intellect, mysteriously financed by government generosity, devoted to training the sons of an educated élite to become just another cultivated élite. [*Shot of* **Childers'** *face. Discomfort.*] It *is* a dream and we've got to wake up. What we need is a new breed of academic and a new breed of students. People who are more interested in the real world than in what Schopenhauer thought about free will. Universities are part of the modern world, and the sooner they realize it the better. Universities like this one have dedicated themselves to inter-disciplinary studies, audiovisual systems, new techniques of teaching, new relations of subjects. They are democratic . . . in their way. But are they relevant? [**Flora**'s *expression: surprised approval.*] I suspect talk about standards and values is a way of hiding the fact that we're doing very little. An ivory tower university hasn't a hope in hell, these days, of doing anything, getting anywhere. [**Flora**'s *face: shifting to disapproval. She catches* **Childers'** *eye. He is plainly uncomfortable.*] But a university involved with commerce, working with industry, will not only serve society. It will learn from it; earn from it. [**Childers'** *face. Hating all he hears, he is rooted to his chair by proprieties.* **Flora** *whispers to* **Patterson**.] Our job, as much as industry's, is to see that this country produces more, more efficiently, with a minimum of waste. [**Flora** *talks to* **Patterson***: she is indignant.*] Universities should cease to be finishing schools for vacillating liberals and immature Marxists . . .

At this point **Flora** *ostentatiously gets up and leaves. Her eye catches* **Childers**. *He is acutely embarrassed. He looks away. As she walks down the aisle, we see one or two other people leaving. But no more than a handful.*

Over her departure, **Good**'s *speech continues; the following lines cover her arrival at the door and outside.*

Good: We should offer a lead to the country. What we need are schools of business studies; of futurology, plotting the nation's future. We should teach practical skills. We should be producing language-trained businessmen for Europe. Advanced computer programmers. Advertising copywriters. Men and women who can transform our society and get us past economic stalemate.

8 Outside the lecture hall

We see the door of the lecture theatre. It is closed. Suddenly it opens. **Flora** *comes out. She slams the door behind her and leans back on it.*

Flora: The man's a shit!

Fade.

9 Outside the lecture hall

The platform party coming through the doors. **Good** *is lighting a cigar. They are joined by* **Gaynor** *and* **Helen.**

Gaynor: Very good, Professor Good.
Good: Thank you.

Childers *appears with* **Helen.**

Helen: Hello, darling. You looked terribly solemn.
Childers: A mildly disturbing occasion.

Humbolt, *the vice-chancellor, takes off his hat and robes and hands them to the* **registrar.**

Humbolt: Excellent occasion, Good. Meet my wife, Mrs Humbolt.
Good: Ah, how do you do.
Gaynor: We'll see you for dinner tonight, I think.
Good: Yes, indeed.
Gaynor: And there's a Mrs Good.
Good: There is. Over there. She's been off fighting architects.

In the distance we see a Jensen Intercepter waiting: **Lee-Ann Good***, a gamine-type, sitting at the wheel.*

Gaynor: Until this evening. It's just a small dinner party. A welcome.

Good: We'll look forward to it. Well, I must get on.

Good *crosses to the car and gets in.*

Gaynor: I'll say this for you, Humby. You're improving.

Humbolt: I'm glad to hear it.

Gaynor: I thought you only appointed professors on the principle they were fifty-four and had trench mouth. But this one's handsome.

Humbolt: Well, we try to please everyone, my dear. He's rather a catch, you know. Not sure myself I like him. But I like one thing. He'll lift this university into a better league altogether.

10 By the paternoster

Flora: Why in hell's name did you just sit there?

Childers: But, Flora, you can't just walk out.

Flora: I did.

Childers: I was on the platform. Besides which, just because I didn't agree with him . . .

Flora: Oh, God: on the one hand this, on the other hand that. Six of one, half a dozen of the other. You should have stayed at Oxford. At least nobody there would notice if you drifted into a coma.

Childers: Flora! [*Pause*] I suppose you're not going to dinner at the VC's, then.

Flora: Of course I am. Do you think I'd pass up a free meal and a fight? Undermine them from within. Besides, I want to see Humbolt operate.

Childers: Operate? Really, Flora, you do have the strangest notions. Remember, I know the man, I went to college with him. We overlapped at Oxford.

Flora *steps into a paternoster compartment.* **Childers** *has to bend down as she vanishes from sight in order to catch her last words.*

Flora: Just because you went to bed with his wife once you don't have to spend the rest of your life doing penance.

Childers *looks around at the students who have heard this. To escape he steps quickly into the paternoster, remembering, too late, that he has left his briefcase on the floor beside the lift. As he vanishes from view we hear his despairing cry*

Childers: My briefcase!

We see him then from another floor as he plunges downwards, a worried expression on his face. And we hear his voice from the next scene.

Childers: The weakness of liberalism being, you might say, its chief virtue.

11 The lecture theatre

Childers *is lecturing. We see that the issue is real and alive for him. For the students, who are taking notes in a desultory way, it is simply exam fodder.*

Childers: To see both sides of a question is to risk being frozen into inaction but it is also the gift of recognizing contradiction, tension, complexity without ceasing to function. The liberal is a man of conscience, but a man whose conscience is a real force in the world. He must be able to act.

12 The students' cafeteria

The sound of **Childers'** *lecture continues as we see him in the cafeteria. The effect is a contrast between what he is saying and the fact that he is patently overwhelmed by the simple task of getting* his meal. *Accordingly, he forgets his bread roll and tries to change his main course while the queue erupts around him. He has to go back for his knife and fork.*

Childers: . . . The liberal view gives you command over yourself and your environment. It enables you to find your way through the real and fundamental problems of the modern world without trembling.

We now hear the full sounds of the cafeteria as **Childers** *walks uncertainly across to a table, balancing his tray and with four pound notes in his mouth, his change from the cashier.*

*   **Flora** *and* **Patterson** *are sitting at one of the tables.* **Flora** *has finished eating and smokes a miniature cigar.* **Patterson** *is eating spaghetti and cheese.*

Patterson: Professor Childers!

Childers *comes over and puts down his tray.*

Patterson: Are you eating those or is it some kind of trick?

Childers *takes the pound notes out of his mouth.*

Childers: Oh, hello, Patterson. Flora. May I join you?
Patterson: Fine. Sit down.
Childers: What on earth's that?
Patterson: Cheese and spaghetti.
Childers: Do you like it?
Patterson: Not particularly. It's supposed to be binding.
Childers: Binding?
Patterson: I've just been abroad. For the British Council. Now I only need to get a letter from them for my bowels to liquefy. Flora says you're going to the VC's tonight.
Childers: Does she?
Patterson: So am I. Dining with the nobs. I suppose

32

it's because I'm the token underling on development committee. I gather it's to welcome our new Professor Good. I hope he's not as awful as his lecture.

Childers: You didn't like it?

Patterson: I can't say I look forward to seeing the Queen's Award for industry flying from the university flagpole.

Childers is struggling to open a can of beer.

Flora: Here, give me that.

Flora opens it easily.

Childers: Thank you, Flora.

Patterson: You should have heard Flora on about it just now. The language.

Childers: Like all sociologists, Flora subscribes to the conspiracy theory of history.

Patterson: Oh, that's not sociology, that's paranoia. I expect she got it from all those pre-pubescent conspiracy books. *The Secret Seven. Five Go A-Caravanning.* With me it was always *Biggles Flies.*

Flora: And what's Biggles flies?

Patterson: You know. *Biggles Flies North, Biggles Flies Nor-Nor-East* . . .

Flora: What I fail to understand is how a scholar, an historian, who wrote the classic work on the break-up of feudalism, can't see the historical forces at work in the ascendancy of Professor Benjamin Good.

Childers: Feudalism had the advantage of being relatively simple. Things now are a trifle more complex.

Flora: A typical historian. You people raise hindsight to the status of a profession. An empty longing for the past.

Patterson: [*Holding aloft a strand of spaghetti*] Nostalgia isn't what it used to be.

Flora: Look, Mark. There are people in this university who are looking to you for a lead. Are you going to give it?

Childers looks surprised.

Childers: What kind of a lead?

Flora: Isn't it obvious? Ever since this university started our vice-chancellor has succeeded in pleasing everyone. Promising the conservatives tradition, the radicals revolution. Never too far, this way or that. Now he's going too far. Selling the place to commerce. The radical faculty will back you. It's time for confrontation.

Childers: Honestly, Flora. Do you see me waving a banner? Shouting non-negotiable demands?

Flora: No, Mark. I can't say I do. But you could leave.

Childers: Leave?

Flora: Resign. With maximum publicity.

Childers: Is that fighting?

Flora: It could be.

Childers: I'll think about it. I'll make my position clear.

Flora: If you ever find out what it is. Excuse me. I have a class.

Flora gets up and walks purposefully away. **Childers** *half gets up, out of politeness.* **Patterson** *continues to play with his spaghetti.*

Patterson: Flora's great walking-out day.

Childers: She scents the great moment. Of course, in a way, she's right. It's the start of the cash-and-carry university. But what good would my leaving do?

Patterson: Oh, I'm sure Flora has worked it all out. A

Childers defence committee. A Childers sit-in. A call for an inquiry.

Childers   I'm not sure I want to be used in other people's revolutionary games.

Patterson: Oh, she means it for your good, too. She thinks revolt is therapy. Oh, God, excuse me. I've got to go to the toilet. See you tonight.

Childers: Yes.

Patterson: Help yourself to the cheese, if you fancy it. The spaghetti's cold.

We see a close-up of **Childers'** *face as* **Patterson** *leaves, amidst the bustle of students in the cafeteria.*

13 The vice-chancellor's house: his bedroom

It is evening.

A Georgian dressing mirror: in it we see **Gaynor Humbolt** *drop a dress over herself; an elaborate dress, slightly outrageous in colour and neckline, certainly 'artistic'.* **Gaynor** *is in her middle forties, dramatic, aggressive, splendid. As the shot widens during the speeches, we will see that she and* **Humbolt** *are dressing for dinner.*

Tension throughout the scene. **Gaynor**, *who has had one drink already, another gin on hand in the bedroom, is a reluctant hostess. One detects an air of irresponsibility which deepens as the evening continues.* **Humbolt**, *though a dignified, authoritative figure, is also uneasy. The evening is crucial: he has to get its tone and texture exactly right.*

Humbolt   [*out of vision*] It was a difficult decision.

Gaynor: Of course.

The shot widens to show **Humbolt** *putting on his trousers.*

Humbolt: But I finally picked a '61. Chateau Latour.

Gaynor: [*Straightening her dress*] There. How's that look?

Humbolt: Splendid. I suppose it's formal enough?

Gaynor: [*Turning, aggressive*] What do you mean,

Humby? It's not the uniform of the Welsh Guards
But I'd call it formal, wouldn't you?

Humbolt [*Dry*] I simply wondered whether the rati‹
of bosom to dress was right for the occasion.

Gaynor: As I understand it, the occasion's to welcom‹
our new professor. I'm welcoming him.

Humbolt: To welcome him, Gaynor, not smothe‹
him. He's a professor. Not some ridiculous painte‹
with earrings and . . .

Gaynor: [*With an attempt at dignity*] That ridiculou‹
painter was a talented artist. Whom I helped.

Humbolt: Much as I believe in subsidizing talent
dear, you might have left it to the Arts Council
They do it with that bit more decorum.

Gaynor: You think so.

Humbolt [*Buttoning his shirt*] I do. Good will give u‹
our chance to catch up. Then even you might com‹
to like it.

Gaynor: And you'd still deny him my top slopes.

Humbolt: [*Tying his tie*] He's not a skiing instructor
Gaynor. Charm. And tact. On the whole, th‹
Welsh Methodist virginal simper would be prefer‹
able to the Tiger Bay tart's grin. We do want t‹
keep him.

Gaynor: [*Putting on her eyeshadow*] Ho ho.

Humbolt: There's one thing, though, Gaynor. You
might keep an eye on Mark tonight. He seems ‹
little put out.

Gaynor: Because he *is* a little put out. You screwe‹
him, and he's a little put out.

Humbolt: Mark indulges himself. You might jus‹
soothe him down. As only you know how.

Gaynor: [*Turning to face* **Humbolt**] Humby, I've tol‹
you. I have no influence on Mark. I've not seen him
for half a year. The truth is he's as dull as the rest o‹
you.

Humbolt: You didn't always think him dull.

Gaynor: Humby, you're a cheap blackmailer, and eventually people will realize. And you can't keep playing the same cards, over and over. Don't your staff know the games you play?

Humbolt: [*Innocently*] Games, Gaynor?

Gaynor: Win Good, lose Mark. That's fair.

Humbolt: Oh, I need them both. I'm not going to lose Mark.

Gaynor: No? Well, I'll have no part. I'm tired of this place. And your petty academic politics. And I'm going to fry my own fish tonight. Christ, why don't you pack it in?

Humbolt: [*Surprised*] Pack it in?

Gaynor: What is there to being a vice-chancellor these days? In a university that never got properly started? The government shoots you down financially. The students shoot you down politically. You groan in your sleep. You don't even enjoy it.

Humbolt: But I do, Gaynor.

Gaynor: Politics without power. Go back into diplomacy. Now that I liked. Or go back to London; and play games that really matter.

Humbolt: [*Putting on his jacket*] Oh yes, Gaynor. Now, what games would you play?

Gaynor: I'd paint. I had the offer of a commission today. In London itself.

Humbolt: May we not have London tonight? It may surprise you, but I like it here. We'll make something of this struggling place. Good's changed everything. I thought he interested you.

Gaynor: You'll not keep me here with him. Humby, your fly's undone. [*She zips it up*] A little thought?

Humbolt: [*Putting a rose in his buttonhole*] What's that?

Gaynor: If Mr Good is really such a big fish, and he's rescuing you from the financial doldrums to the tune of half a million, now, where does that leave you?

Humbolt: The head, for the first time, of a large and thriving university.

Gaynor: No, Humby. Second fiddle.

Humbolt: I don't think so.

Gaynor: Second fiddle. You've *no* grip on *him*. If he's going to give, he's going to take. And from what I hear and see, he's no Mark Childers, to be pushed around by appeals to truth and justice and honesty and all those old ladies.

Humbolt: I'll handle Good.

Gaynor: And not lose Mark?

14 Childers' house: a bedroom

Helen and Childers *are dressing for dinner: a contrast to the last scene. Their bedroom is heavy north Oxford style, likewise* Helen *and* Mark. *She sits at the dressing table in a rather nondescript, dark dress, fixing her pearls. He buttons up an ancient dress shirt, complete with cuff links, and then puts on a decidedly dated dinner jacket. There is an impression of shabbiness, but of a fairly intimate relationship between the two.*

Helen: I suppose Gaynor won't mind seeing this dress again.

Childers: It should give her a feeling of security.

Helen: I wonder what she'll wear. Little Mrs Good. Why is he called a whizz-kid?

Childers: Well, a whizz-kid's a very smart sort of person who invents projects. Mr Good invents projects.

Helen: What's he do when he's invented them?

Childers: He goes round the organizations that support research. Foundations, government departments. And he says, with marvellous conviction: for fifty thousand pounds I can solve the mystery of the universe.

Helen: And at that price they take it.

Childers: Not just like that. No, they say: Professor Good, we've studied your project with interest. We like the idea of solving the mystery of the universe. It's just up our street. However, we wonder if you could include something on the effects of smoking on unborn children. We know it's not your field. But no need to do the research yourself. Get a team. That will up the price a bit, but we thought it was low anyway. So he comes home to his university, which is naturally very pleased with him, and gives him leave from teaching, which is something of a chore for whizz-kids, to have a bash at the universe mystery.

Helen: And you needed someone like that here.

Childers: Oh, _I_ didn't, Helen. Humby did. Good's hardly my cup of tea.

Helen: But Humby always consults you.

Childers: Well, this time he didn't. Good was appointed last term. When I was in Rome.

Helen: Couldn't they have waited? You weren't gone long.

Childers: No, I wasn't, was I? But if they'd waited, I'd have objected. Then they'd have had no whizz-kid.

Helen: You've advised Humby on all academic matters. It's abominable.

Childers: Money's short in higher education. A VC gets desperate, especially if he's first and foremost a politician, like Humby. I should, in his shoes. His action makes utter sense. It's just morally wrong, that's all.

Helen: We've known Humby for a long time. I'm going to tell him what I think of him.

Childers: No, Helen.

Helen [*Getting up*] Do I look a frump?

Childers: No, not really.

Helen [*Laughs*] I see now why you don't charm th foundations.

Childers: How would you like to go back to Oxford

Helen: [*Staring at him*] What? Seriously?

Childers: I had the offer of the Finesburg Fellowship

Helen: You did? Well, I'd like it. But would you Aren't you committed? Haven't you . . . too man ties?

Childers and Helen now have their coats on, and are goin towards the door.

Childers: Have you seen my car keys? No, no ties .

Helen: It's utterly up to you, Mark. *You* must decide But won't Humby try to stop you?

Childers: How? How can he?

15 Outside the vice-chancellor's house

We see a bicycle arriving: it is **Patterson**. *He gets off, puts hi bike against the railing. He mounts the steps and rings the bell. Hi lips round in a soundless whistle.*

16 The vice-chancellor's house: the hall

The **steward** *opens the front door.* **Patterson** *stands on th step, wearing his raincoat and bicycle clips. Behind the steward a* **waitress** *hovers with a drinks tray.*

Patterson: Hello.

Steward: What name, sir?

Patterson: It's Dr Patterson.

Steward: May I take your coat, sir?

Waitress: [*Coming forward*] Sweet or dry, sir?

Patterson takes a drink and then tries to take his coat off. In th midst of this tangle, a shot up the stairs shows **Humbolt** *an* **Gaynor** *descending.* **Gaynor** *carries a drink. It is a terrifying sight from* **Patterson**'s *point of view.*

Humbolt: [*Loudly from the stairs*] Hello, there. [*Nearer*] Ah, Mr Patterson, isn't it?

Patterson: That's right.

Humbolt: This is Patterson, my dear. My wife.

Patterson, *with his coat half-off, a drink in one hand, attempts to shake hands.*

Patterson: How do you do, Mrs Humbolt.

Humbolt: Mr Patterson is in, er, English; that's right, isn't it?

Patterson: Absolutely. Very good.

The **steward** *helps him off at last with his coat, so that he stands there in his Burton's suit, still, however, wearing his bicycle clips.*

Gaynor: Well, now. Come on through and entertain me. You and I shall start the party.

Patterson: Am I the first? Shall I go away and come back later?

Humbolt: Nonsense, Patterson. Come into the drawing room and tell us all about yourself. There'll be reinforcements in a moment.

17 The drawing room

It is later. This is a biggish room, clearly used for public as well as private purposes. The party is under way. The **waitress** *circulates. Everyone has arrived except the* **Goods**. *We catch snatches of conversation.*

Childers: Helen's been off all afternoon, prison visiting.

Gaynor: Must all seem very familiar after university teaching. Especially here. What do you think of thingy, the new wonder boy?

Childers: Have you met him?

Gaynor: Not really. All I got was multiple fractures of the fingers when he shook hands and a quick blast of Old Spice.

Childers: Flora thinks he's anti-Christ.

Gaynor: [*Looking at* **Childers** *more closely*] Flora?

Childers: [*Slightly embarrassed*] Flora Beniform. Over there.

Gaynor: Oh, yes. Of course. Well, from what I hear of Dr Beniform her theological credentials are a little dented. But what do you think of him?

Childers: I rather fancy he's the kind of man who thinks that euthanasia is a logical expression of the aspirin.

Cut to:

Helen: Haven't you been abroad or something? For the British Council?

Patterson: Yes. The person they asked couldn't go.

Helen: How was it? Were they interested?

Patterson: I suppose so. They asked all kinds of questions.

Helen: Questions?

Patterson: Yes. Like, was George Eliot by Adam Bede or Adam Bede by George Eliot. And what were the six important things about Macbeth. And was it true that all contemporary writers were homosexual.

Cut to:

Childers: This is Flora Beniform.

Flora: Hello, Mrs Humbolt.

Gaynor: Oh, Dr Beniform. I've heard lots about you.

Flora: It's pleasant to have such a reputation.

Gaynor: Mostly shocking things, actually. [*To the passing* **waitress**] A gin, please, Mary.

Waitress: Yes, mum. With tonic.

Gaynor: Gin. [*Holding two fingers apart*] Like that. You're in physical education, I gather.

Flora: Social psychology.

Gaynor: That sort of thing.

Flora: They're different sorts of things. In physical education they box. My line's concealed aggression.

Childers: Flora works on the family.

Gaynor: Ah, ha. Are you married?

Flora: No.

Gaynor: Shouldn't you be? I'm sure you could get a research grant for it. You can get a research grant for anything, as far as I can gather. There's a man in biology who grinds up lizards' testicles.

Flora: Marriage isn't necessary. You don't have to be schizoid to be a psychiatrist.

Gaynor: Really. Humbolt's father was. Both.

Childers: I thought he was a butcher.

Gaynor: No. He was a psychiatrist who thought he was a butcher. How does one work on the family anyway?

Flora: Well, one just watches. Watches and listens and notes.

Gaynor: In my day they called that voyeurism.

Flora: Probably they did. In your day.

There is a pained silence.

Childers: Ah, here come the royalty.

*The **Goods** stand in the doorway. **Ben** has a change of suit. **Lee-Ann**, a very smart American, wears an expensive fur coat. Between them is slung a carrycot.*

*The **steward** comes in with them. We see **Humbolt**'s face: for once he is nonplussed, by the baby. He hurries towards them.*

Humbolt: Ah. My guest of honour. Come in.

Good: [*Confidently*] Hello there, Bartley.

Lee-Ann: [*Brightly, looking round, to everyone*] Hi, everybody. I'm Lee-Ann Good.

A small pause. **Gaynor** *comes up.*

Humbolt: My wife, Gaynor.

Lee-Ann: Hello, Mrs Humbolt.

Gaynor: I see you've brought the family.

Lee-Ann: Do you really mind? We couldn't get a sitter. And I have to breast-feed her later.

Gaynor: No, fine. Mason: there's a baby.

Steward: Yes, ma'am. It could go upstairs in one of the bedrooms.

Lee-Ann: Oh, that would be just dandy. She sleeps anywhere.

Gaynor: You come with me. I'll find a nice spot for you to leave him.

Lee-Ann: She's a her, Mrs Humbolt.

Good: Let me take it.

Lee-Ann: No, Ben; you stay here and socialize. You're the one they want to meet. I'll manage. [*To* **Gaynor**] Okay?

In the background conversation has been resumed. **Gaynor** *leads* **Lee-Ann** *from the room.*

Steward: [*To* **Good**] Your coat, sir.

Good: Oh, thanks. [*To* **Humbolt**] Sorry if we're a bit late. We're doing demand feeding.

Humbolt: Oh.

Good: [*To* **steward**] Oh, just a minute. [**Good** *takes a package from the pocket of the coat the* **steward** *is holding. To* **Humbolt**] It can be pretty inconvenient. Coming over in the plane . . .

Humbolt: [*Edging* **Good** *forward into the room*] Oh, yes, you've been in Europe.

Good: Well, we're all in Europe. [*He gives* **Humbolt** *the package*] I brought you a duty-free bottle.

Humbolt: Thank you.

He is at a loss with the package.

Waitress: [*To* **Good**] Sweet or dry, sir?

Good: [*To the* **waitress**] Ah, that's just the job. Thanks, my dear.

As he picks up a drink, **Humbolt** *pops the package on the tray.*

Humbolt: Now, come and meet some people. You know Mark Childers.

Good: Yes. Nice to meet you again.

Childers: Yes. How are you liking it here?

Good: Oh, very well. You're off to a good start.

Childers: You think so.

In the background, **Lee-Ann** *and* **Gaynor** *have returned into the room.* **Lee-Ann** *is in a stylish American suburban costume, say fashionable party trousers and lurex top. The ladies now form a group, talking together.*

Good: Sure. And now we go for the big league. [*Feeling he has done his duty by* **Childers***, he is now looking across at the ladies*] Well, I'd better meet some more people. Why don't I go and entertain the ladies?

We see **Childers**' *reaction, then cut to the ladies:* **Lee-Ann, Flora, Helen, Gaynor.**

Lee-Ann: This is a really great house you've got here.

Gaynor: Do you think so? I hate it. [*To the* **waitress**] Honey, bring me another healthy gin.

Waitress: Yes, Mrs Humbolt.

Gaynor: And easy on the tonic.

Lee-Ann: We're looking for something sort of big. [*To* **Good***, as he joins them*] Aren't we, honey?

Good: Right. Hello.

Helen: You've not found anywhere yet?

Lee-Ann: Oh, boy, I mean, have you ever *tried* moving house in England? I mean, the system's really against it. The electric outlets are all different sizes,

the dishwasher won't fit the space for the dishwasher, the eye-level grill is level with someone
else's eye . . .

Some laughter

Flora: You've moved a lot.

Lee-Ann: I'll say, three times since we came from the
States. Ben never settles.

Flora: Oh, really?

Good: I've been looking for the big opportunity. Now
I've found it.

Flora: [*To* **Lee-Ann**] But how do you feel about
that?

Lee-Ann: Me? It's Ben's career.

Flora: What about *your* career?

Lee-Ann: Oh, she's upstairs in her cot, sleeping.

Flora: But your *career*.

Helen: She means, don't you *do* anything. We all do
something here.

Lee-Ann: Really? Like what?

Helen: Gaynor paints, and helps at the family planning
clinic . . .

Gaynor: Toulouse-Lautrec, the vasectomy queen of
Mercia.

Helen: Flora's a full-time academic, and I teach at the
prison.

Lee-Ann: Well, that's great. You realize yourselves.
And Ben agrees, don't you, Ben, he's very progressive . . .

Flora: Is he?

Lee-Ann: He says I can work if I want.

Good: That's right.

Lee-Ann: But I just feel that when a man's going right
to the top he needs a wife who's supportive.

Flora: Which leaves you powerless.

Lee-Ann: No, it's what I want.

Flora: We'll have to liberate you, Mrs Good.

Lee-Ann: Look, I'm fine.

Good: Lee-Ann does just what she wants.

Flora: Repression exists because its victims choose it.

Gaynor: Mrs Good, we're not just an empty head on top of two tits.

Lee-Ann: I guess not.

Gaynor: Some of us aren't, anyway. How about some dinner?

18 The dining room

A row of wine bottles stands on the sideboard: four white and six red, already uncorked. The **steward** *picks up a bottle of white wine and adjusts a napkin round the neck. He carries the bottle to the table where the guests chat. Again we hear snatches of conversation, though on occasion the whole table listens to a particular exchange, especially when* **Gaynor** *wants her husband to hear.*

*   **Gaynor** *has arranged the guests as follows:* **Humbolt** *at the head, with* **Good** *on his left,* **Helen** *on his right.* **Gaynor** *is at the foot of the table with* **Lee-Ann** *on her left,* **Childers** *on her right.* **Flora** *sits between* **Good** *and* **Childers***, and* **Patterson** *between* **Helen** *and* **Lee-Ann***.*

*   *The* **waitress** *is serving soup. The* **steward** *goes to* **Humbolt***'s end of the table.*

Humbolt: Well, Helen, how are the children?

Helen: Bartley . . . we don't have any.

Humbolt: Oh, Helen, that's right.

The **steward** *pours a small quantity of wine in* **Humbolt***'s glass. He tastes it, holding it in his mouth and pushing it against his lower lip. A serious ritual.*

Humbolt: Very good, Mason. [*To* **Good**] It's a [*Whatever the wine is: A good one*]. I think you'll like it.

Good: I'm not a wine man.

Humbolt: You'll learn.

Good *turns to the soup.*

Good: I'll tell you one thing that impresses me about this place, vice-chancellor. The buildings.

Humbolt: Very fine, aren't they? We have a Dutch architect. Piet van der Krank, a very visionary fellow. Wanted to build the whole place standing in water. We had to stop him, of course.

Good: They're frankly modern. I like that.

Now we hear the conversation at **Gaynor***'s end of the table.*

Gaynor: [*To* **Lee-Ann**] Well, tell me, my dear. What do you think of us?

Childers: You must give her time, Gaynor. She's only just arrived.

Gaynor: [*Her hand is on* **Mark***'s arm: the index finger of her other hand is held to her lips in exaggerated gesture*] Ssshhhh. I want a . . . virgin impression.

Lee-Ann: Well, okay, I'll give you an impression. I really think I'm going to settle here. It's such a nice quiet place. I hope that's not just American sentimentality.

Gaynor: Oh, it's splendid. The knife-grinder comes once a fortnight, and the man from the Census calls every ten years, to see if anyone's still living here . . .

Childers*' face registers sadness and concern, seeing the discontent under the jokes.*

You know what the action-packed headline in this morning's local paper was? Yoghurt Farmer Fined for Dung-Splashed Walls.

Lee-Ann: But you're all such good company for each other.

Gaynor: Mrs Good, if you were Einstein and he [*pointing to* **Childers**] were the Bolshoi Ballet, it would still be what you Americans call the sticks. If you gold-plated the Finefare, and started *chemin de fer* in the cathedral, it would remain the backend of nowhere. Not a fit place for a creative person to live in.

Lee-Ann: [*Amused at what she takes to be witty tabletalk*] Anyway, it must be wonderfully healthy, out here in the country. Fewer coronaries.

Gaynor: [*Looking pointedly at her husband*] Don't knock coronaries. They're all we women have got to guarantee us a prosperous and exciting middle-age.

Fade down.
Fade up on the **waitress** *collecting the empty prawn cocktail dishes.*

Humbolt: Of course the ambassador was delighted. He's never seen black pudding before.

Helen: What happened?

Humbolt: He served it, for some high dignitary – I think it must have been the Austrian Foreign Secretary. A solemn occasion, anyway. What's this, asks this chap. Yorkshirewurst, says his excellency . . .

Helen turns to **Patterson**.

Helen: What were you lecturing on in India?

Patterson: Harold Pinter and the failure of communication.

Helen: How did it go?

Patterson: I don't know. They didn't seem to understand a word I said.

Fade down.
Some time later. Fade up as the banter begins to give way to rather more serious and bitter exchanges. The bottles of white wine have all gone. The **steward** *picks up the first of the red, and wraps the*

neck. The **waitress** *is serving the pheasant. The* **steward** *takes the wine to* **Humbolt** *and stands by his side.*

Humbolt: Ah, Mason [*to* **Good**]. This is the Latour I was telling you about.

The **steward** *pours a little into* **Humbolt**'*s glass. The ritual again.*

Humbolt: You must taste this with care, Good, old chap.

The **steward** *takes another bottle of wine to the table.*

Flora: [*to* **Patterson**] What does Isobel do when you're off in the Orient?
Patterson: She hibernates. Hangs from the roofbeams by her toes.
Flora: Leaving her to the nappies.
Patterson: Have you never heard of Napisan and the automatic washing machine? They don't bash them on the rocks any more, you know.
Flora: That's charming, Andrew. Have you ever asked yourself why you need to repress her?
Patterson: I don't repress her. She could do what she likes. But there are people who like football, or drink, and people who like popping babies out of themselves. She'd do it even if I never went near her. She'd find a way.
Flora: A typical male response.
Patterson: Typical! What kind of a word is that? How many people do you know with habitual dysentery and a wife whose culinary education began and ended with 'e' is for egg?

Lee-Ann *turns to* **Gaynor**.

Lee-Ann: I guess with your interest you have to go to London a lot.

Gaynor: Which of my interests did you actually have in mind? Young men? The theatre?

Lee-Ann: [*Beginning not to know quite how to handle Gaynor*] You paint, Mrs Humbolt.

Gaynor: Oh, *those* interests. No, I don't paint. I am *a painter*. That is my profession, which I profess. When I am not entertaining at table.

Lee-Ann: I'm sorry.

Gaynor: I don't just paint. I exhibit.

Lee-Ann: Where can I see your work?

Gaynor: In the galleries. In our nation's capital, which I am not allowed to mention.

Lee-Ann   You're not?

Childers: [*Restraining her. He doesn't want her to make a fool of herself or hurt anyone else*] Gaynor!

Gaynor: I am not. Humby doesn't like it. [*She raises her glass*] Humby!

Humbolt: [*Raising his*] My dear.

Childers: There are times when Mrs Humbolt misses the bright lights.

Gaynor: You know what I miss, Mark? The passion for doing anything. There was plenty when we started, we were going to irrigate the desert, make Oxford feel like Southend-on-Sea. What happened? The appeal fell flat, we started too late, the architect spent everything building buildings on stilts, the students started sitting in, everyone got scared . . .

Childers: We've achieved a great deal.

Gaynor: And the bright brilliant people, here they are, got tired. They dressed out of the boutiques, and they screwed the wives of their colleagues, their serious contribution to radicalism and relevance. And now you've come. I think you're definitely our type. You look bright and promising. So we'll charm Mr Good, and take his half million,

51

and then he'll get tired too, and so it goes. [*Raising her glass*] So there you are, honey, welcome to Mercia.

Lee-Ann: Nobody beats Ben. Ben doesn't give up.

Childers: Gaynor's feeling disenchanted. It's not like that. I still have passion.

Gaynor: God, Mark, passion? I tried it. That's passion?

Lee-Ann *is confused.* **Childers** *is hurt. He looks at* **Gaynor**.

Gaynor: Passion, he says. Don't let that glint in the eye deceive you. Here's a man who gave up Oxford to come here. Levi-Strauss sat next to him at dinner every night. He drank wine all day. Here he is now. Tired. Lost.

Childers: Gaynor, please!

Gaynor: No armchairs. No Levi-Strauss. He oozes disappointment.

Childers: I came here to do what I wanted to do. And I've done it.

Lee-Ann: What was that?

Childers: To create an open, enquiring university for open, enquiring students. To spread educational opportunities. To develop my subject.

Gaynor: Come on. What would it take to bring you alive again?

Childers: Gaynor.

Gaynor: Take me to London tomorrow.

Childers: London? Tomorrow?

Gaynor: You see? What passion? You know what Humby wants from me. And you. Compromise. A subdued demeanour. While Mr Good takes over. Let's run.

Lee-Ann: [*Laughing*] Oh, you're joking. Ben doesn't want to take over anything. He's much too nice.

Gaynor: Yes, I am joking, Mrs Good.

We see **Childers'** *reaction. Fade out.*

Fade up on side table. The bottles of red are now empty. The **waitress** *is clearing the main course plates.*

Good: Well, look, take an example. A company decides it wants a new factory. They go to an architect. What do they get?

Helen: A building?

Good: Right. Alternatively, they come to my project team. Now what do they get?

Flora: *Not* a building.

Good: No. They get a future projection.

Patterson: How nice. Does it keep the rain out?

Good: They think they want a factory. But do they? On what theory of growth, what model of technological evolution? Their needs can be quite different. A new product. A new tool. A new frame of reference.

Flora: A divorce. A new hairstyle. This is just vulgar, old-fashioned psychoanalysis applied to industry.

Good: Aren't you the lady who walked out of my lecture?

Flora: I believe I am.

Good: Might I ask why?

Flora: I didn't like it, you see.

Good: Why not?

Flora: I have a low tolerance for capitalist claptrap.

Good: Ah, you're a radical.

Humbolt: [*Anxious to cool things*] One of our nicer radicals.

Good: You see, you misunderstood, Dr Beniform. I want to see this country changed as much as you do. Good heavens, I *was* born in Sheffield Brightside after all.

Flora: I don't care if you were born in a stable. I know capitalist pragmatism when I hear it.

Good: But you didn't *stay* to hear it. I'm saying that real change depends on new thinking, not on out-moted nineteenth-century sloganeering.

Flora: I simply happen to believe in change through Marx and Engels, not through Marks and Spencers.

Good: Dr Beniform, if you want social change, you don't get it through revolutionary gestures. You get it out of advanced industrial development.

Flora: That's the oldest trap in the business.

Humbolt: Then what's your answer, Flora?

Flora: The answer is that people like us, people in universities, ought to break out of it, by putting other questions first. Questions about the rightness of the entire industrial system.

Good: There's no breaking out of it.

Flora: There is. Perhaps we should sit down with you, give you an overview. A new product . . .

Patterson: A new tool . . .

Flora: A fresh frame of reference.

Humbolt: [*Affably dismissive*] Oh, come now, Flora. I think you're missing the point.

Helen: I think Mark is too, Humby. You could lose him, you know, with this.

Humbolt: Oh, come now, Helen, I need Mark. You tell him so. Just as I need Ben . . .

Good *is not mollified.*

19 The hall

*The **waitress** carries an impressive dessert through into the dining room.*

We follow her into the room.

20 The dining room

Humbolt: [*In relief*] Ah, dessert. [*To **Gaynor***] Change ends, my dear.

Humbolt *and **Gaynor** ceremonially rise and go round the table,* *n order to change places.* **Gaynor** *sits next to* **Good**, *still angry.*

Gaynor: [*To* **Good**] It's called host-swapping. Like wife-swapping, but you can do it at meals.

We see **Good**'s *irritable reaction.* **Humbolt** *next to* **Lee-Ann.**

Humbolt: [*To* **Lee-Ann**] The British ambassador always changed ends, when I was British Council Representative in Vienna. As he said, it mixes the pot.

Lee-Ann: Vice-chansh . . . vice-chancellor . . . I just have to ask you. Do you always eat like this? By yourselves?

Humbolt: [*Patting her arm*] Oh, we put on something a little special for the Goods.

Lee-Ann: It's a really ducky meal.

Humbolt: [*To* **Childers**] Well, Mark, how's history?

Childers: Evolving.

Humbolt: I've just been talking to Good about the history of future studies. I want a word with you about the future of history studies. How's the centre?

Lee-Ann: Are you planning a centre, Professor Childers?

Childers: I was.

Humbolt: An admirable scheme for a centre of Victorian industrial studies. It's aroused international interest.

Childers: And no cash.

Humbolt: Is that why you're thinking of leaving? Helen said you were.

Childers: No, not that.

Humbolt: Is it serious, Mark?

Childers: Yes.

Lee-Ann: Just when we've come?

Humbolt: I'll not have it. Who'd restrain Mrs Good's

husband if you went? Doesn't he need it, now and
then, Mrs Good?

Lee-Ann: [*Giggling*] I guess he does.

Humbolt: You thought I'd forgotten you, Mark,
didn't you? You're wrong. I've thought of your
interests throughout.

Childers: Have you really, Humby?

Humbolt: You'll see. Later. [*To* **Lee-Ann**] Am I
being appallingly rude?

Lee-Ann: Oh, no, you're charming.

Cut to **Gaynor** *and* **Good**: **Good** *is deep in the dessert.*

Gaynor: Do you like eating, Mr Good?

Good: I do.

Gaynor: Dinner is for conversation. You can always
snatch a bite to eat between meals.

Good: Do you like entertaining, Mrs Humbolt?

Gaynor: Why not Gaynor, Ben? Oh, I'm an enter-
tainer, all right. On the grand scale. But I do have
other talents.

Good: I'm sure you do.

Gaynor: I'm an artist. I create. In fact I've just
received a commission to work on a new arts centre
in [*whispering*] London. Humby doesn't approve.

Good: Humby?

Gaynor: [*Nodding towards* **Humbolt**] Him. He. That
one. At least, he won't when I tell him. He's very
suspicious of real artistic talent, you see. The envy
of the thinker for the doer. [*Pause*] I'll bet you're a
doer, Ben. You certainly strike me as a doer.

Good: I suppose Professor Childers is a thinker.

Good *suddenly leans over the table.*

Good: Professor Childers . . [**Childers** *looks up*] I
gather you disapproved of my lecture.

Childers *is embarrassed at being forced into a dinner-table confrontation.*

Childers: Well, in all honesty, I thought it had everything to do with cash and nothing to do with education. I'm an old-fashioned liberal . . .

Good: Ah, there's the problem. Liberals haven't got us very far, have they? You know what they say; if God had been a liberal, we wouldn't have had the ten commandments. We'd have the ten suggestions.

Childers: I'm sorry: I'm afraid for me education has something to do with civilization.

Good: Well, you have a choice, Professor Childers. You face it here. You can be traditionalist. Put up a few buildings that look as though they were built in 1350 or so. Have a handful of port-drinking faculty teaching theology to students who say 'orf' instead of 'off', and regard themselves as the hereditary rulers of the nation. Or you can try something modern and daring. For which purpose, as I understand it, you appointed me.

Childers: As it happens, I didn't appoint you. Had I not been out of the country, had I not, I suspect, been manoeuvred out of the country . . .

Humbolt: Oh, Mark!

Childers: I would have voted against your appointment. Yes, there's a choice. Between an independent, humanistic university, and a place where the vice-chancellor is appointed by the CBI, and our main task is research on the development of the plastic kipper.

Good: Professor Childers: that's ignorant parody.

Humbolt: Gaynor.

Gaynor *knows this signal: she stands up.*

Gaynor: Well now, ladies . . .

Helen *rises, knowing the convention.* **Flora** *sees the point and rises slowly.* **Lee-Ann** *remains seated.*

Helen: Are you coming, Mrs Good?
Lee-Ann: Where are we going? Home?
Helen: We must leave the men to talk of manly things.
Flora: While we go and bitch in the drawing room.

Lee-Ann *gets up.*

Lee-Ann: [*To* **Humbolt**] Oh, boy, I feel quite dizzy.

As the ladies leave, **Lee-Ann** *turns in the doorway.*

Lee-Ann: Do I get Ben back after?

The four men are left at the table. **Humbolt** *gets up, throwing his napkin carelessly on the table.*

Humbolt: I thought we'd take port in my study. Come through, gentlemen.

They walk through into the study.

21 The drawing room
The ladies enter, followed by the **waitress** *with coffee.*

Lee-Ann: [*Gushing*] Oh, I'm so sorry, Mrs Humbolt, I just didn't know what was happening back there. I guess I'm not used to your foreign customs.
Flora: Nor am I, Mrs Good.
Gaynor: That's Humby. He keeps up the old decencies.
Lee-Ann: [*Collapsing on sofa*] I want to tell you, Mrs Humbolt. That was really . . . quite a meal. But you know, I can tell, I really can, this is a pretty radical place.
Helen: Not especially. We had one sit-in last year.
Lee-Ann: You did? What about?
Gaynor: The students objected to the university's policy about their sleeping together.

Lee-Ann: What did you do? Expel them?

Flora: Oh no, not at all. We can hardly deny them the consolations of the flesh. We don't deny ourselves.

Gaynor: There's only one cinema in town. They've got to have something to do. Even if it's only each other.

Helen: The real problem was balancing the residences' account. Two to a room, you see. If we find a student's sleeping regularly with someone, we send them a double bill.

Lee-Ann: Actually, what I mean was, *you're* all so radical.

Flora: Isn't that rather a strange word to use of a group of women talking in one room while the men talk in another? Most of the people here talk new, new, new, but they're to the right of Attila the Hun.

Lee-Ann: No, you're wrong. You're emancipated. Not like me.

Flora: Oh yes. Twenty years of education, moral tuition, perseverance and honest toil, and we're all responsible women. Prepared to tackle the major problems of the age. Ready to meet our husbands right in the middle of the intellectual arena. So long as the Avon lady doesn't call, or we aren't too busy selling each other Tupperware for five per cent commission. As half our faculty wives do.

22 The study

The study is a small room with a fireplace. Four chairs are placed round the fire, next to each chair is a small table, with fruit or nuts on it. A holder containing two decanters is by Humbolt's chair. Throughout this scene we must be aware that Humbolt is acting tactically, but his tactics are even more complex than Childers, who is attuned to Humbolt, manages to realize.

Humbolt: Now then. Sit on my left, Good. Mark on

my right. Patterson, you're port boy. [**Humbolt** *has put* **Patterson** *between* **Good** *and the fireplace, so that he will have to pass the port across to* **Childers**. *All are now seated.*]

Humbolt: Well, I'll start this.

Humbolt *pours himself a glass of port and passes the two decanters on to* **Good**.

Good: What is it?

Humbolt: [*Tapping tops of decanters*] Port. Madeira. A good one; you'll like it, Mark.

Humbolt: Nuts, Good.

Good: Pardon?

Humbolt *is holding out a bowl of nuts.*

Good: Oh, thanks.

Humbolt: Patterson, pass the port.

Patterson *passes the decanters across to* **Childers**.

Humbolt: The pears are particularly succulent, I'm told. Well now, Good. Welcome! Here's to you!

Patterson: Cheers!

Good: Thank you. You've been very nice.

Humbolt: Of course, you scarcely come empty-handed. Half a million in grants, project money. I'm not a money man myself. But it means something, these days.

Childers: Evidently.

Humbolt: Yes, it does, Mark. And even to you. I've got some news for you. The almonds are particularly delicious. Professor Good and I have been talking a lot about his proposed centre for future studies. He came up with an interesting thought.

Childers: He did?

Humbolt: Are there some minty chocs over there, Patterson?

Patterson *passes the chocolates.*

Humbolt: Thank you, my boy. I think you should report this, Ben.

Good: The vice-chancellor explained to me your plan for a centre in Victorian industrial studies. I gather it's created quite a lot of academic excitement.

Patterson: It has.

Good: One of our programmes in future studies – it's been financed mainly by oil and transportation sources, I can tell you who if you're interested – is a projection of industrial growth, to the year 2000. We'd take in ecology, sociology, energy sources, mass transportation techniques, housing problems, and needs, you know, the whole thing. Now my point was, this ought to have a well-financed historical dimension, going back to the Industrial Revolution. I've seen your centre plans. I see many of these areas are in it. I thought there was a possible . . . marriage.

Childers: With my centre?

Good: That's right.

Humbolt: In short, we get both developments from one set of funds. We can't afford two separate centres. We can amalgamate. And that, for you, has one enormous advantage. Ben has the money lined up now.

Childers: You've examined my scheme and think you could work with it?

Good: As far as I can see it's completely complementary. It would give my work roots.

Humbolt: And you freedom to develop your ideas.

Childers: It's a big surprise, Humby.

Humbolt: I told you, I'd not forgotten you. Patterson, give the fire a poke, would you, old chap?

Childers: I'd given up on that centre, you know.

Humbolt: But it matters to you, doesn't it.

Childers: Oh, yes.

Humbolt: I'm not rushing you, Mark. But as soon as you can give me your provisional assent . . .

Childers: I'd have to look at it carefully.

Good: Well, no great rush.

Childers: It's very tempting. Look: am I right in thinking that this money's in the form of attached grants and we'd be working on commissions?

Good: That's it.

Childers: Give me an example. Something we could jointly do.

Good: Well, we've a commissioned study of the decline of the nuclear family, with support from the Social Science Research Council.

Childers: Yes, yes; that would be possible.

Good: Then there's the problem of social control. That's another interesting area. The Home Office has asked us to do a study of mob behaviour. [**Humbolt** *sees this is inept.*] Now there's an obvious historical dimension to that.

Childers: [*Sensing the catch*] The Home Office?

Humbolt: That's one of many options. You'd have rights of choice over projects, of course.

Childers: There may be obvious historical dimensions. But isn't there an obvious political one as well?

Good: The aim is a scholarly, multi-disciplinary study.

Childers: In crowd control.

Humbolt: It would be premature at this stage to consider specific projects. What we need is some decision in principle.

Childers: In principle! With schemes like that? The Home Office? You call that 'principle'?

Humbolt: Forget that, Mark. It was a bad example. Think of the advantages.

Childers: I'm thinking you're trying to buy me.

Humbolt: Don't be ridiculous. You'd be independent.

Childers: You're trying to buy my support for projects I'd be bound to oppose in every committee in this university – on academic grounds as well as on moral grounds. As far as I can see, Humby, you're about to shift this university in a new direction, a wrong direction, for purely cash reasons. While all I've done here, all the academic values I stand for and you used to, go by the board. No, Humby.

Humbolt: Patterson, you're on Development Committee. Isn't this the answer to growth we've been looking for?

Patterson: Who, me? Well, if you'd like my opinion . . .

Childers: They'd be mad to touch it, Humby.

Humbolt: That's a false judgement, Mark. I think this is academically right. And, as you well know, history applications have been falling. Whether you like it or not, students are demanding some contemporary relevance in their studies.

Childers: Of course, they'll love to hear we're going into business with MI5. I can see that getting unanimous support in the Student Union.

Humbolt: That's a red herring, Mark. The Home Office project was just one suggestion.

Childers: Oh, it's more. It seems to me to be symptomatic of the worst kind of academic pragmatism.

Humbolt: That's ungracious, Mark.

Childers: Ungracious?

Humbolt: To Professor Good.

Good: No, I understand. You fancy yourself as teaching the moral alphabet to adenoidal High Church homosexuals from Eton and Harrow en route to the foreign office. And what do you think they've got tucked away in their moral consciences? Their vision of paradise is a balance of payments surplus and occasional emasculation of telephone box vandals, carried out by private doctors. You're underwriting an educational system that produces people dedicated to selling out every principle you claim to believe in.

Childers: I simply refuse to side with efficiency and the power élite.

Good: Cliché. It's just that my stuff's not your idea of education. The bright young man's not your idea of a civilized person. But it is education, Professor Childers. What I'm doing. It has method and purpose. And, frankly, your cooperation would not be a favour. It might help you – advance your work, advance your mind. But your mind's too dead to see it.

Childers: Some things are worth fighting for.

Humbolt: Then stay and fight for them. You've been the moral conscience of this place, Mark. We can see that matters, even when disagreement occurs. What you must accept, Mark, is that I have to give some thought to the future. To change and growth. To our image.

Childers: Image! We're not film stars.

Humbolt: It's just that we need money, energy, new blood.

Childers: Humby, this is a university, not the Coal Board. You'll have my resignation in the morning.

Pause.

Humbolt: I wonder, Good, Patterson; would you mind leaving us? Joining the ladies?

Childers: It's no use, Humby.

Humbolt: Thank you, gentlemen.

Good *and* **Patterson** *leave.*

Humbolt: That didn't sound very well, Mark.

Childers: It wasn't meant to.

Humbolt *stands up and throws nutshells in the fire. Pause.*

Humbolt: You know, Mark, I don't think you understand this, but I'm a serious man. I have to be the
politician, and you know the odds I'm up against
now. Don't you? Mr Good is necessary to this
place. He may not be nice. I don't always expect to
agree with him. But think of it, Mark. If you were
VC – and thank God you're not – how would *you*
keep us going?

Childers: I'd cut my coat according to my cloth.

Humbolt: There's no bloody cloth, Mark. We need
Good. We also need to contain him. He's got stuff
up his sleeve I know nothing about. And you're
right, there's a risk of outside interference. We
need a watchdog.

Childers: Yes, you need me. He's got so much financial strength he could run the place. Run you. But
you've bought him now.

Humbolt: At a price, as you see. I do share many of
your fears.

Childers: That's not all the price. You've divided the
faculty. As never before. Sound them. You've got
trouble ahead.

Humbolt: Which I counted on you to help me
with. You're the essential item. I must have you,
Mark.

Pause.

Childers: I'm sorry, I'm not a fool, Humby. You
destroy what matters, and then want me to bail you
out. But you'll not hold me here like that. I feel the
responsibility: not to you, to my colleagues, many
of whom I brought here.

Humbolt: Well, how shall I hold you, Mark? Do you have some terms?

Childers: No, no terms. I leave you to the problems you've created. As no doubt others will.

Humbolt: There's no appeal I could make?

Childers: None at all.

Humbolt *walks away from him.*

Humbolt: You surprise me. I never thought of you as self-interested. A man who made trouble and then left it.

Childers: Made trouble?

Humbolt: You've built up support. If you go, you'll divide us totally. A university's a fragile construct. One man can break it if he means to. As you clearly do.

Childers: You're playing with me, Humby.

Humbolt: I'm not. I've stopped persuading. I'm just a little appalled.

He takes **Childers** *by the arm.*

Humbolt: So be it. Let's join the ladies.

23 The drawing room
Humbolt *and* **Childers** *enter the room. The ladies, with* **Good** *and* **Patterson***, are drinking brandy.*

Lee-Ann: Vice-chansh . . . vice-chancellor . . . I'm having a great time. [*Holds up her brandy glass*].

Humbolt: Are you, Mrs Good? Wonderful.

Gaynor: Humby! Welcome to purdah.

Lee-Ann: Oh, Mr Humbolt, you must be proud of your wife.

Humbolt: I am, Mrs Good, I am. In what way?

Lee-Ann: Her creativity. Her being an artist, and all.

Humbolt: Ah, she's been explaining her part-time activities, has she?

Gaynor: Some of them, ducky, some of them.

Humbolt: Why not all? You should have heard everything. We're all very proud of Gaynor. Her probation officer. Her psychiatrist . . .

Lee-Ann: But you don't understand her, vice-chancellor.

Humbolt: My dear Mrs Good. I've been married to Gaynor for twenty-five years. A certain understanding comes . . .

Lee-Ann: Twenty-five. What anniversary's that?

Gaynor: Tin, Mrs Good, tin.

Flora: Is twenty-five years of marital struggle really a good lesson in human nature?

Humbolt: The best.

Lee-Ann: Are you against marriage too?

Flora: What's wrong with fornication?

Childers: Helen, we've got to go.

Helen *looks across at him.*

Humbolt: Oh, come, Mark, stop for coffee. The staff have gone. But I'm sure Gaynor can turn her artistic hand to coffee-making.

Gaynor: I can?

Lee-Ann: Hey, come on, let me help.

Humbolt: Oh, shouldn't we get the male into the kitchen?

Flora: It would be a step in the right direction.

Humbolt: Who shall we send? Which unreconstructed male?

Gaynor: [*To* **Good**] Come on, we'll go and grind some beans.

Flora: [*Going over to* **Childers**] Mark, what did you do?

Childers: I resigned.

Flora: That's marvellous.

Childers: [*Blankly*] Yes.

Flora: And did he take it?

Childers: He asked me to stay.

Flora: Look at him. Don't.

24 The kitchen

There is a general clutter of dishes and glasses, left by the staff to clear next day. We see **Gaynor***'s hand as she stubs out a half-smoked cigarette in a dish of shrimp cocktail.*

Gaynor: Another drink, Ben.

Good *holds up his glass in an ironic gesture.*

Good: I've still got some brandy. Pass the port.

Gaynor: Pardon?

Good: Pass the port. I never thought I'd hear, not in a progressive new university, I never thought I'd hear anyone say 'pass the port'.

Gaynor: Humby may be progressive, but he's not a man to let outmoded customs die just because the world's moved on a century or so.

Good: Not my style, I admit.

Gaynor: No. You're here to transform us. [*Looking him in the eye*] What about it, Ben Good?

25 The drawing room

Throughout the following scene we stay with **Childers** *as he moves round. The important thing is his reaction to what's said: his sense of the pain beneath the banter. He is shaken, almost shattered, by his interview with* **Humbolt**.

   Humbolt *approaches* **Flora** *and* **Childers***, brandy glass in his hand.*

Humbolt: Well, Miss Beniform. An interesting evening for your research?

Flora: It has its insights. But I'm used to shrill marital pairs. Being in a department that specializes in them.

Humbolt: What, social studies? How about the Kelleys? A delightful couple. I'm very fond of them. Excuse me: I've something to see to.

Flora: He won't see much of them this week. They're divorcing.

Patterson *approaches.*

Patterson: Who's divorcing?
Flora: It's all right, Andrew. Not you.
Patterson: I didn't think it was. But you never know here, do you?

26 The hall
Humbolt *stands in the hall, holding his brandy. The door of the kitchen is slightly open. He sees* **Good** *and* **Gaynor** *kissing. He raises his glass slightly and turns back towards the drawing room.*

27 The drawing room
Childers *joins* **Helen**, *who is talking to* **Lee-Ann**.

Lee-Ann: Oh, Professor Childers. What a marvellous party. Your wife was telling me about all the marvellous sexy things you do.

Childers *looks blank.*

Helen: I was talking about the latest round of swaps. Benita Pream's gone to live with Leo Bennett, in physics.
Lee-Ann: And has she children?
Helen: Two. *And* she's taking on Leo's three.
Lee-Ann: I think that's brave. What about her husband?

We see **Humbolt** *coming in at the door. He comes towards this group.*

Helen: Oh, he's moved in with Dorothy Zweig. In social studies.
Lee-Ann: What about Mr Zweig? Is there one?
Helen: He's decided to become homosexual.
Lee-Ann: Oh, boy, I love you all. God, am I bushed!

Lee-Ann *subsides on to the settee.*

Childers: Is she all right?

Humbolt *joins them.*

Humbolt: I'm afraid we've all drunk rather a lot. Well, Helen; has Mark told you he's leaving us?

Helen: No. [*To* **Childers**] You've resigned.

Childers: Yes.

Humbolt: It's a tragedy.

Helen: One you've made, Humby. If only you'd consulted him first.

Humbolt: Helen, there is my version. [*He puts his arm round her shoulders*] Don't you think you ought to listen to it?

Childers: Isn't it best for us to go?

Humbolt: No, Mark. I don't want Helen to go like this. You were waiting for coffee. Pop into the kitchen and hurry Gaynor up. I want to say something to Helen.

Childers: It makes no difference, Humby.

28 The hall

Childers *comes out of the drawing room and shuts the door behind him. He stops. There is sweat on his face. He wipes it off with a handkerchief. He hears something: the noise of the baby, crying upstairs. He looks up the stairs. He walks along the hall towards the kitchen door.*

29 The kitchen

Good *and* **Gaynor** *are kissing. The shot is from behind* **Good** *and towards the kitchen door, which stands part-open.*

 The noise of the crying upstairs is audible.

Gaynor: Good, Good, very good.

Childers *appears at the kitchen door. He opens it wider. He stops. A brief reaction shot of his face: surprise and shock.*

Then a shot from his viewpoint: **Good** *and* **Gaynor**, *with* **Good** *facing towards him. Now* **Good** *sees* **Childers**, *his eyes staring over* **Gaynor**'s *shoulders. He is caught, and he knows it.*

Childers *hovers: politeness makes him wonder whether to leave, indignation makes him want to stay. He steps forward.*

Childers: That's your baby crying, Professor Good.

Gaynor *turns. The clinch breaks. She is not concerned.*

Gaynor: Whoops.

The baby cries more loudly.

Good: Isn't Lee there? What can *I* do? It needs ten minutes at the breast.

Gaynor: A taste she shares with others.

Childers: Your wife's asleep.

Good: Asleep? She can't drink a lot.

Gaynor: Go on, nursemaid.

Good: Where's Lee now?

Childers: On the sofa in the drawing room.

Good *goes.*

Gaynor: Oh dear. Caught with my hand in the cookie jar.

Gaynor *is at the mirror, fixing her face.*

Childers: He's appalling. He's personally dangerous. Do we need a man like that?

Gaynor: What brings you to the party?

Childers: I was sent to hurry you with the coffee.

Gaynor: Hell, Mark, the coffee. They must be drinking the water out of the vases. There's a bag of beans in the cupboard behind you.

Childers: [*Opening the cupboard*] This one?

Gaynor: That's it. Can you use a coffee grinder?

Childers: I think so.

Gaynor: Very good. There it is.

Childers *tries to grind the coffee, while* **Gaynor** *fixes the percolator.*

Gaynor: Sent? Who sent you?

Childers: Humby.

Gaynor: Ah, Humby.

Childers: That man's obscene beyond belief.

Gaynor: Humby?

Childers: No.

Gaynor: Oh, wonder boy. Well, he definitely failed to satisfy the examiners. Not a great performer, Mark.

Childers: It's not just his principles that appall. It's his empty human style.

Gaynor: What's that to you? You're leaving, aren't you? And you're right. Get out, before you're eaten up.

Childers: He'll not eat me up.

Gaynor: Not by *him*, he's child's play. By all these messy, miserable, fouled up people you consort with, and want to rescue. The way you want to rescue me. Don't you? You always were a masochist, Mark. I thought I taught you that lesson.

Childers: A masochist with principles.

Gaynor: [*Coming over, watching him grind the coffee*] God, Mark, not like that. You look like a hurdy-gurdy man. Let me.

Gaynor's *hand pushes* **Childers**' *off the coffee grinder. They are close to each other. He looks at her. She gives him a peck on the cheek.*

Gaynor: You were better, even you. Go on, Mark. Go home.

Childers *goes to the door.*

Childers: That bloody man. Why, Gaynor?

Gaynor: He's all right. You know, you scared him. Caught him with his trousers down. Metaphorically speaking. A nastier man could destroy him with that.

Childers: Yes.

Childers *turns to go.*

30 Outside the vice-chancellor's house
The guests are leaving: **Childers** *and* **Helen**; **Flora**; *the* **Goods** *with their carrycot.*

We catch a glimpse of **Humbolt** *in the doorway, and hear shouts of good night and cars starting.*

31 The drawing room
The room is empty. We hear the outside noises of departure.
Gaynor *enters. She sees the brandy bottle and pours some. She sits down.* **Humbolt** *comes in.*

Humbolt: Well, that's that.

Gaynor: What I call a real party. Blood and guts all over the wall.

Humbolt: [*Pouring a drink*] A lively evening.

Gaynor: You sent Mark to the kitchen.

Humbolt: [*Innocently*] Yes. I wanted a private word with Helen.

Gaynor: Humby, I'm leaving you.

Humbolt: What?

Gaynor: Leaving. L,E,A,V, ING.

Pause. They look at each other. Then, incredibly, **Patterson** *comes wandering in. They have both forgotten him. They stare in surprise.*

Patterson: I'm dreadfully sorry. I'm afraid I've been sick. In some kind of cupboard.

Humbolt: Patterson!

Patterson: I think it was a broom cupboard. There was no bloody light. Never made it to the . . .

Similar thing happened at my first lecture. It was terrible. A big lecture. Three hundred of the little buggers, all sitting there. I walked down to the front and I was nervous, desperate for a pee. I saw this door. I went in. It was a broom cupboard, with a self-locking catch. I stopped there until everything went quiet. Twenty minutes. Then I chucked myself at the door. Fell out on my face and all three hundred of them burst out laughing. They knew. They'd just sat there quiet, waiting for me to come out. [*Pause.*] Where's everyone gone?

Humbolt: Home.

Patterson: Home?

Gaynor: Home.

Patterson: Oh, I say. I'm dreadfully . . . I must be going myself. I'm terribly sorry.

Humbolt: Don't let it worry you, Mr Patterson. I'll show you out.

32 The hall

Patterson *is putting on his coat.*

Patterson: I'm awfully sorry about the cupboard.

Gaynor: Good night, Mr Patterson. Mind how you go.

Gaynor *turns and goes slowly upstairs.*

33 The bedroom

Gaynor *lies on the bed, balancing her glass on her forehead.* **Humbolt** *comes in and begins to take off his tie.*

Humbolt: So you're leaving me?

Gaynor: Yes. [*Pause*] I had a call today. From London. I've got a commission from the Holborn Arts Centre. They said there could be more.

Humbolt: But you don't have to leave, Gaynor. You could do it from here.

Gaynor: I can, but I shan't. I want . . . to . . . go. I'm fed up. Tired of bra-less students fornicating for socialism, and faculty with rising damp. And especially tired of you. I'm tired of being your instrument. University equipment. Depreciating annually. Set against tax. Used to maximum capacity. And I'm especially tired of being used in your games.

Humbolt *undresses calmly.*

Humbolt: Now what games, Gaynor?

Gaynor: I don't know and I don't care. I'm going to London and I'll find myself a flat or a penthouse and that is the end of you.

Humbolt: There's no appeal I could make?

Gaynor: None at all.

Pause. **Gaynor** *sits up.*

Gaynor: Was there a game?

Humbolt: A game?

Gaynor: Oh, for Christ's sake, stop playing around. Was there a game tonight? There was, wasn't there?

34 Inside Childers' car
The car is an old Rover. **Childers** *is driving, very inexpertly.* **Helen** *sits next to him in the front.* **Flora** *is in the back.*

Helen: It says stop. That means you stop. [*Turning round to* **Flora**] What did you think of the new folk? Nice company.

Flora: Yes. He's a social fascist, and she's a suburbanized zombie. But they sat up and ate nicely.

Helen: I suppose that's our last visit there. Mark's leaving.

Flora: Is he really?

Helen: Humby said you wouldn't.

Childers: Why did he say that?

Flora: He knows you.

Childers: Flora: you have a very interesting field of research.

Flora: My families?

Childers: When the coloured races have taken over, and the world's different, probably not better, they'll remember these times for two things.

Flora: Which?

Childers: Our liberal ideals of freedom and conscience; and our belief in family life. What they'll not know is what knotted messes we got ourselves into on both counts.

Flora: That sounds like an excuse.

Childers: For what?

Flora: You're not leaving, are you, Mark?

35 The vice-chancellor's bedroom

Gaynor: There was, wasn't there?

Humbolt: A very small game.

Gaynor: I was in it.

Humbolt: I thought you were very good.

Gaynor: It was Ben, wasn't it? That's who you fixed.

Humbolt: No one was *fixed*, Gaynor.

Gaynor: Poor old Ben.

Humbolt: Hardly poor. With half a million.

Gaynor: But tarnished in the kitchen. Still, Humby, you lost Mark.

Humbolt: Maybe. But I wonder. We want him to stay, don't we?

Gaynor: We? You do. I'm going. Remember?

Humbolt: Because of this silly commission.

Gaynor: That just makes it possible. I'm going because you've used me up.

Humbolt: But it's such a small commission. An abstract mosaic. Five thousand pounds. You can't last long on that. Not in a penthouse.

A long pause as Gaynor realizes the significance of what he's said.

Gaynor: How did you know that?
Humbolt: Let me see. Initial sketches by March. Final designs by the following October.
Gaynor: [*A final realization*] You!
Humbolt: Me.
Gaynor: It's not true.
Humbolt: No? Ring them. Ring Henry Thompson, the director.
Gaynor: Henry Thompson? [*Getting up in anger*] You lousy sod. You set it up.
Humbolt: I shouldn't have mentioned it. I never intended you to know.
Gaynor: Just to give me a glimpse of freedom, and then shut the door again.
Humbolt: It was a small gift, a present.
Gaynor: Just to get me to lower my guard.
Humbolt: Not at all. Happy twenty-fifth wedding anniversary, my dear. I hadn't forgotten.

Pause. Then **Gaynor** *begins to laugh.*

Gaynor: Humby, you're a swine, how do you do it, how do you take me in? But why? There has to be a reason.
Humbolt: I did it all for love, Gaynor, all for love.

Gaynor *looks at him, sinks back on the bed and closes her eyes.*

Humbolt: So you'll stay.

Gaynor *doesn't answer.*

Humbolt: Oh, by the way . . .
Gaynor: Yes, Humby.
Humbolt: I was thinking, tomorrow night, don't you think we ought to get Mark round?

Gaynor: Mark is going, Humby. You may keep me, you won't keep him.

Humbolt: Oh, I don't think he'll go. I think his ire's roused now, he'll want to stay and fight Ben Good. Let's just have him by himself. Smooth his ruffled feathers. You will be there, won't you, Gaynor?

Gaynor: It bloody looks like it, doesn't it? But why?

Humbolt: I need you, Gaynor. I'm just no good at these things. You're so much better at them than I.

36 The vice-chancellor's office, at the university

An echo of the sequence at the beginning. A shot past **Humbolt**'*s shoulder down on campus.* **Childers** *is walking down the university path. The camera slowly zooms down onto him as he walks along. In a separate shot we see* **Good** *behind him. As we hear its closing music, we see both of them enter the paternoster. As the credits roll they pass the various floors in the lift.*

LOVE ON A GUNBOAT

Love on a Gunboat was first shown on BBC1 in the 'Play for Today' series on 4 January 1977, with the following cast:

Leslie Potter	Stephen Moore
Monica Potter	Barbara Flynn

In 1976:

Fay Scace	Josephine Welcome
Hamish	Andrew Downie
Elaine	Mikel Lambert
Group Leader	Terence Taplan

In 1956:

Dennis Horncastle	James Hazeldine
Dora Horncastle	Arwen Holm
Forcett	Gerard Ryder
Mr Potter	Denis Holmes
Interviewers	Christopher Coll, Julian Fellowes
Knitting Lady	Jane Freeman
Mr Biffen	Bernard Gallagher
Nun	Julia McCarthy
Mrs Bone	Christine Ozanne
Bus Conductor	John Salthouse
Jazz enthusiast	Lloyd McGuire

Script Editor:	Pedr James
Designer:	Michael Edwards
Producer:	David Rose
Director:	Robert Knights

1 Newsreel collage (1956)

Clips from black and white newsreel films:

A débutante's party in 1956. Just enough to show the social and class distinctions, also the fashions and styles.

The explosion of the Bikini Atoll hydrogen bomb.

The visit of Bulganin and Khrushchev to England in spring, 1956.

During these clips we hear rock and roll music and other popular hits from the period.

2 A Birmingham underpass (1976)

Coming out of the darkness of a Birmingham ringway underpass, into modern television colour, is an MGB sports car, top down, of recent but not new registration.

The driver of the car is **Leslie Potter**, *just over forty, a journalist on a local paper. His style is men's shop smart: denim safari suit, shirt open at the neck displaying a medallion, a full fashionable haircut. His looks will contrast markedly with those in the later 1950s scenes.*

A reverse shot from within the car as it comes out from the darkness into the day. A burst of light. Then upward shots from the car of the busy street scene, high-rise buildings, Birmingham's modern towers, the Rotunda and the Post Office Tower: the Second City skyline.

3 Newsreel collage (1956)

Film of:

An American comment on British action in Suez.

Bulganin and Khrushchev at Karl Marx's grave in Highgate Cemetery.

Marilyn Monroe with Arthur Miller.

4 School entrance, Birmingham (1976)

The dark overshadowed entrance of a school. Figures are moving beyond the glass doors. A door opens, and **Monica Potter** *comes out, holding a* **child** *by the hand and talking to it. She carries a large bag with books in it.*

Monica *is, like* **Leslie**, *just over forty; she is dressed in reasonably smart but not at all stylish clothes.*

She comes out into the sunlight.

Cut to:

5 Birmingham street (1976)

Leslie's car drives off the street and down into an underground car park. Leslie is next seen running up a staircase. He crosses the reception area of a big modern newspaper office, filled with people.

Leslie goes through the journalists' main area, where the typewriters clatter and the staff work, towards:

6 The editor's office (1976)

Hamish, the editor of the paper, is at his desk.

Hamish: Come in, Leslie. I was reading your feature lead.

Leslie: Nice to know someone does.

Hamish: Do they?

Leslie: Oh, ho.

Hamish: [*Picking up paper*] Aura, is that right, photography: a glimpse of our undreamed of powers.

Leslie: That's it. A special camera. People in intense or psychic states cause sparks on the print. Lovers emit flashes.

Hamish: I read all that. Do you think it's a big turn-on in Nechells, Leslie?

Leslie: The occult. There's a universal obsession with the occult.

Hamish: Not in my family. Look, Leslie: what's your lead tomorrow?

Leslie: The bee. The remarkable powers of the bee.

Hamish: The bee?

Leslie: Bees have an extraordinary intelligence. And an advanced welfare state.

Hamish: I thought they left their workers to die.

Leslie: There you are then.

Hamish: I'm not very impressed, Leslie. I look through your page, there are no bloody people on it these days.

Leslie: I'm in my abstract period. [*Pause*] Okay, I'll rethink it.

Hamish: Right, you do.

Leslie: [*Looking at his watch*] Excuse me. I think I've got an angle on a social problem story.

Hamish: That's better.

7 A Birmingham back street (1976)

A busy, poor back street in Birmingham. In the crowds, walking towards us, we see **Fay Scace**. *She is twenty-four, a social worker. She is modernly dressed in a blouse and a denim suit. But where* **Leslie**'s *clothes are Boutique,* **Fay**'s *look radical-efficient. She is carrying files or a documents case and has a working professional look.*

She comes round the corner of a dress shop and walks towards the camera.

8 Another Birmingham street (1976)

From the sports car, we see Leslie's view of Fay as she turns the corner. He waves and stops. Fay hurries up to the car and gets in.

Fay: Leslie.

Leslie: Fay. Good, great, you made it. How's things?

Fay: [*As the car starts*] All right. No, shot really. I shouldn't have left her.

Leslie: Who's that?

Fay: Oh, this case. I'm sure she's harming that child. It's a familiar form of psychic transference.

Leslie: That's all right, then.

Fay: She justifiably hates her female role. She identifies the child as the cause of the role. So she harms it. How are you?

Leslie: Not so good. I haven't beaten anybody for weeks. Dave Brubeck. [*He indicates the radio.*]

Fay: [*Looking round*] Who?

Leslie: Dave Brubeck. A jazz star of the fifties. Very very intellectual, was Dave Brubeck. [*His hand is on Fay's arm*] Of course you're much too young to remember, love.

Fay: Of course.

9 The White Swan restaurant (1976)

Fay: But what gets me is, why won't she let me help her? I understand, I'm a woman, another woman . . .

Leslie: Maybe she doesn't see you as a woman. Maybe she sees you as authority.

Fay: Don't think I hadn't thought of that.

Leslie: I didn't.

Fay: She stands there on the doorstep. All the time I can hear it crying upstairs.

Leslie: Maybe one reason so many people have so many problems is that there are so many other people with so many solutions.

Fay: That's a very smug remark, Leslie.

Leslie: Yes. I know I'm a swine, but can't we, just for a bit, forget the social work? I mean, we're having lunch together.

Fay: I thought having lunch with you was social work. Christ, Leslie, these prices.

Leslie: The end of the world is nigh. I thought we'd eat first.

Fay: If you ate everything on this menu, how much would it come to?

Leslie: You want to? I'll call the bank.

Fay: It's crazy. Why did you bring me here?

Leslie: I wanted to get you away.

Fay: It's not your kind of place.

Leslie: It's a place where you go for treats.

Fay: I feel like somebody's mistress.

Leslie: I was going to mention that. Let's . . . after?

The wine list descends between them. They look up. **The wine waiter** *is standing above them.*

Leslie: Oh. Hullo. Have you chosen? I thought white-bait and scampi.

Fay: Scampi too. I'll have a steak and kidney pie.

Leslie: A good old English custom. Well, fish and meat, very difficult.

Fay: Oh, dear. The great bourgeois dilemma. White or red. [*To the* **wine waiter**] A bottle of rosé. The great bourgeois solution.

Leslie: I don't like rosé. And I'm not bourgeois.

Fay: No? What do you call you, Leslie? You eat scampi in expensive restaurants. You live in Solihull. You have a BUPA subscription, and a dinghy in the drive. And you're not bourgeois.

Leslie: I'm a fifties liberal. I was famous for my anger.

Fay: Oh? What did you get angry about, Leslie?

Leslie: Suez. Eden's Eden. The zombies and the phoneys.

Fay: And who were they, Leslie?

Leslie: The people who didn't say yes to life.

Fay: But you said yes to life.

Leslie: Of course. If I was asked. Can I come to your flat after? Say yes, it's life.

Fay: Oh, is that what all this is for? No, Leslie. I hate it after a big meal. And I'm seeing a client at three.

Leslie: But you're the only person I can talk to. And it's my bloody big meal.

10 A high block of flats, Birmingham (1976)

From the car park, where the MGB stands empty, the camera pans up to the top of a very high block of council flats. Over this, we hear the voices of Fay and Leslie, in post-coital mood.

Fay: Okay, talk.

Leslie: What about? At the blood transfusion, they give you a cup of tea.

Fay: Bloody hell, Leslie, you talk to me, do you hear?

11 A bedroom, in the top floor flat (1976)

A sparse modern bedroom with radical posters on the walls. **Fay** *and* **Leslie** *are in the bed.*

Leslie: You know, Fay, I do care a lot about you.

Fay: I'm sure you do. It's a very nice arrangement. You've a nice wife you can talk to about your children. You've a nice mistress you can talk to about your wife. Of course you . . .

Leslie: Can't talk. I really do, Fay. It only makes sense now I've got you.

Fay: What would she say if she knew?

Leslie: Monica? I don't know. Nothing. Cry.

Fay: Why?

Leslie: Well, she's not like you. She thinks Freud got it all wrong. It's not sex we're all after, it's Tupperware. Domesticity is Monica's dream. She doesn't bite, she keeps her nightie on in bed, she thinks about the kids, and she sticks to the marriage contract we signed.

Fay: But you find it absurd.

Leslie: Not absurd.

Fay: But not saying yes to life. [*The alarm clock rings on the bedside table*] Come on. Up you get.

Leslie: Fay, stay a minute.

Fay: Next patient. Up you get.

Fay gets out of bed. After a moment, **Leslie** *follows. During the next sequence, they dress in parallel. She puts on her pants, he puts on his, etc.*

Fay: You know, I'm mad to do this with you.

Leslie: No. I need you.

Fay: Oh, I know you do. And I know why.

Leslie: Why?

Fay: To feed your bloody little bourgeois angst. You have this nice safe life, the wife, the kids, the house, the car.

Leslie: The stereo, the boat, the inglenook fireplace.

Fay: You love it and you despise it. So once a week, Thursday lunchtime, good old radical Fay.

Leslie: People do lead lives they never meant.

Fay: Everybody leads lives they never meant. Some people try to do something about it.

Leslie: It's not so easy.

Fay: What *did* you mean, Leslie?

Leslie: Ah, well. I meant to be a writer.

Fay: I thought you were.

Leslie: I'm a journalist. I meant a writer.

Fay: Really. Weren't you any good?

They are dressed, in their similar denim.

Leslie: There's an old saying. In Patagonia there are two poets. The better is called the Patagonian Shakespeare. There are a lot of us around. Patagonian Shakespeares.

Fay: Come on. There's a clean towel in the cupboard. Your comb's still in the drawer.

11 The bathroom of the top flat (1976)

Leslie, *towel in hands, stares at his face in the mirror. He drops the towel and takes the comb from the drawer. In the mirror, we see* **Fay***'s face as she comes in behind him.*

Leslie: You want it to stop.

Fay: It's no good, is it?

Leslie: Of course it's good.

Fay: Karl Marx knew you. A clear case of false consciousness.

Leslie: I knew Karl Marx. A clear case of bourgeois liberalism.

Fay: I don't believe in fidelity, Leslie. Not like Monica. But I don't believe in shoring up your phoney marriage. You're so unreal, Leslie.

Leslie: Everybody says reality as if they knew what it was.

Fay: Well, it's not you, is it, Leslie? There's the reality of people, there's the reality of history, there's the reality of me. Isn't that why you come here? Because I'm the only chance of a real life you've got?

Leslie: Maybe. Yes.

Fay: All right, then. Leave her, move in here. You can. You wouldn't be the only one, but then you don't believe in fidelity either, do you?

Leslie: Move in? Come to you?

Fay: Inconceivable, isn't it? Bloody Patagonian Shakespeares.

The telephone rings out in the hall.

Leslie: Someone's after you.

Fay: Are they? Leave it, I'm late. Drive me down into the city.

Leslie: Fay, you're breaking me in two.

Fay: You're in two already, Leslie.

13 The car, in a Birmingham street (1976)
The MGB moves through the traffic. Modern buildings. **Fay's** *hair blows in the wind.*

14 Central Birmingham (1976)
The car moves slowly down Colmore Row, looking for a place to stop. It halts opposite the graveyard. **Fay** *hugs* **Leslie**. *Then she takes our her comb to comb her hair.*

Fay: Okay, well then, thanks.

Leslie: I'm going to think about it.
Fay: You can't say I wasn't quick. I'm famous for it. Okay, Leslie.

Fay *gets out of the car. A car behind hoots.*

Leslie: Can I see you next Thursday?
Fay: You're blocking the traffic. Telephone me, to-morrow lunchtime. Okay?

Fay *runs off between the gravestones towards the high buildings beyond, the shops and towers.* **Leslie** *stares after her. A car behind hoots, Leslie starts the car and moves out. As we watch his face in the mirror, we hear Fay's and Leslie's voices:*

Fay: But you said yes to life.
Leslie: Of course. If I was asked.

15 The school entrance, Birmingham (1976)
We continue earlier shot of **Monica Potter** *leaving the school with the child. She walks across the tarmac, in animated contact with the* **child***, who runs from her and then back again.*

16 The school driveway (1976)
The MGB stops at the entrance to the drive. A shot across **Leslie** *shows us the tree-lined entrance, which curves away round a corner, so that the school itself is not visible and no figures are in sight. Then* **Monica** *comes round the bend with the* **child***. She sees the car, stops, bends to say something to the* **child***, who runs off. Then she begins to walk in patches of sunlight through the trees towards the car.* **Leslie***, from the car, looks at her. Then we zoom in on* **Monica** *as she walks towards him. Then the shot of her freezes, and we cut to:*

17 The arboretum, Nottingham (1956)
Monica *comes down the path through the arboretum. There is a resemblance to previous scene, but* **Monica** *is about twenty. She is in clothes of the fifties, fairly smart ones: a dress with a pinched-in waist, and a large flamboyant hat. Her hairstyle is sensible,*

*long, straight. She carries a handbag. The impression is of a
'decent' middle or upper middle class girl of decidedly good
background, if with a maverick streak shown in the flamboyance.*

Leslie *comes up the path in the other direction. He is twenty-
one. The clothes dated: perhaps a blazer, somewhat baggy
trousers, a light coloured open-neck shirt. The effect is not neat and
tidy: rather of a Dylan Thomas-ish bohemianism.* **Monica** *walks
towards him. As they pass, he looks at her.* **Leslie** *walks on a
little, after* **Monica** *goes out of shot; then he turns and looks back.
Suddenly, he ducks into the bushes.*

Monica *walks further down the path. She passes a park
bench.* **Leslie** *is on the bench, reading a newspaper. She glances at
him curiously, puzzled. He does not look up. When she has gone,
he stares after her, gets up.*

Leslie *runs downhill, through some bushes, and across the
grass.*

Monica *walks further on through the arboretum.* **Leslie**, *his
head down, collar up, trying without real success to look like
someone else, passes her going the other way.*

18 The birdhouse at the arboretum (1956)

Monica *is looking at the birds. She opens her bag, finds some
bread, and throws it into the cage. She cheeps at the birds.*

Monica: Come on, eat up.

She moves on, rounds a cage. **Leslie** *is there, looking at the
birds with apparent great interest.*

Monica *bends down, cheeps at a bird.*

Leslie: Birds are fascinating.

Monica *looks up at him.*

Monica: What sort's that one?
Leslie: I think it's some kind of [*mumbles*] tit.
Monica: Some kind of which?
Leslie: [*Staring straight ahead*] Tit.
Monica: Oh, tit.

They move on together.

Leslie: These must be tropical.
Monica: They look hot.
Leslie: God, if only we could be as . . . honest and
frank as that. Don't you think the British are too
tied by convention?
Monica: I do really, yes.
Leslie: I say, look. You can get tea over there.
Monica: So you can.

19 The teaplace at the arboretum (1956)

Monica *is sitting at an outdoor table.* **Leslie** *carries a tray
towards her, laden with tea, in old-fashioned pot, cups and saucers,
scones, cakes. The place is otherwise deserted. He reaches the
table.*

Leslie: [*Intense*] What do you *do*? What's your life?
Monica: Me. I'm a primary school teacher.
Leslie: Marvellous. That sounds interesting. Children
are interesting.
Monica: You like children.
Leslie: [*Sensing a danger signal*] Well, I do, but at a
distance.
Monica: Is that enough milk? Actually, to be honest,
it's not very interesting.
Leslie: That's just right.
Monica: What I like is earning my living. Being
independent, on my own.
Leslie: You live on your own?
Monica: I have a bedsitter.
Leslie: Splendid.
Monica: What do you do?
Leslie: Actually I'm a writer.
Monica: You *write*! Gosh.
Leslie: Novels.
Monica: Can I read one? Have you published any?

Leslie: I haven't actually finished it yet. It's rather ambitious.

Monica: Oh, you should. People will want to read it.

Leslie: I will. Given time.

Monica: What kind of novel is it?

Leslie: Rather frank, actually. I'm influenced by Lawrence. Also a Nottingham writer.

Monica: *Sons and Lovers?*

Leslie: You read Lawrence?

Monica: Oh, yes.

Leslie: That's marvellous. What do you think of him? I mean, *really* think of him?

Monica: I think he's . . . very profound about people.

Monica: Don't you think he's life-enhancing?

Monica: Yes, I do, really.

Leslie: That's marvellous. He's very neglected and not really understood.

Monica: I suppose that's the trouble with being a writer.

Leslie: Yes. Exactly.

20 The duckpond at the arboretum (1956)

Monica *and* **Leslie** *are throwing bread to the ducks.*

Leslie: Do you like jazz?

Monica: Some of it.

Leslie: Which of it?

Monica: Quiet jazz.

Leslie: You mean cerebral? MJQ?

Monica: Yes.

Leslie: There's a jazz session tonight.

Monica: Oh, where?

Leslie: A pub. It's hard to find. Not very quiet, either.

Monica: Some loud's all right.

21 The school drive (1976)

Leslie *is in the MGB.* **Monica** *approaches the car.*

Monica: Oh, good, you got away.

She gets into the car. A perfunctory kiss.

Leslie: Good day?
Monica: Yes, very good. One of the kids caught fire.
Leslie: Spontaneously?
Monica: She was smoking a cigarette, and pocketed it when I came in.
Leslie: That must have brightened things up.
Monica: And one of the ESNs who never talks to anyone talked to me. That was marvellous. What about you?
Leslie: Oh, nothing.
Monica: A non-day.
Leslie: I saw Hamish. He said my pieces had no bloody people in them. Hamish likes people.
Monica: Is he right?
Leslie: Shall we go shopping?
Monica: Who has a white comb?

*Monica bends down and picks up **Fay**'s comb.*

Leslie: Oh, someone I gave a lift to must have left it.
Monica: Blonde hair. If I dyed mine, would you like it?
Leslie: We could try.

He starts the car. The car drives off.

22 A pub room (1956)

It is evening. The room is used as a jazz club. There is a Chris Barber type group playing. The number is Mood Indigo. A solo riff. The audience is young and respectful. They sit at the pub tables, listening fairly attentively, as if to a lecture.

*Now we identify a table at the front. **Leslie** is there with **Monica** and friends. **Monica** is notably overdressed in a cocktail party type dress ('you didn't tell me'). The friends are: **Dennis Horncastle**, a rather worn and middle aged young man, in loose* sweater and baggy trousers; his wife **Dora**, in plain and ordinary clothes; and **Forcett**, a solemn, critical young man, hopeful of being another Leavis, who smokes a large pipe.

The riff ends to solemn applause from the audience. **Monica** is late to join in. The number continues as:

Monica: [*Low, to* **Leslie**] They don't dance.
Leslie: [*Low*] Nobody dances.

Monica listens for a moment. Then she turns to **Horncastle**.

Monica: It's more like a church service.
Horncastle: [*Amused*] It is a church. The church of St Christopher Barber.

Monica listens for another moment. A pause.

Monica: I'd like another drink.
Leslie: Better wait till this is finished.
Monica: If you go now, there's no one at the bar.
Leslie: All right. What would you like?
Monica: Gin and lime, please. Not much lime.
Leslie: Dora?
Dora: [*Hushed*] Pint, please.
Horncastle: [*Hushed*] Same for me.
Forcett: [*Hushed*] Yes.

Leslie moves through the audience to get to the bar. There are hostile looks. Just as he reaches the bar, the number stops. Applause. Then crowds push savagely round him.

Dora: Has he got enough money?
Monica: Is he really a writer?
Forcett: We are all writers. This *is* Literature.
Monica: Golly. All of you.
Horncastle: [*Pointing to* **Dora**] Not her.
Forcett: You might say we're a school.
Horncastle: The Nottingham School. The Trent's answer to Tolstoy and Dostoyevsky. Leslie's the

novelist, extraordinary gifts. Very good at darning, too. I'm a poet. Forcett's, well, a critic, you might say.

Forcett: You should say. Clear, analytical mind.

Monica: Yes.

Forcett: What we need, indubitably, is a magazine. The creative energy's more than manifest; what's absent is a platform. We live in an age dominated by the metropolitan socio-intellectual clique. The Bloomsbury twitter. The Oxbridge flutter. The BBC bicker. The *New Statesman* mutter. Don't we?

Monica: Yes.

Dora: Dennis, he wants you.

Leslie's *hand waves pathetically from the crowd around the bar.* **Horncastle** *pushes his way over.*

Dora: Actually, they're all on grants doing PhDs.

Enthusiast: Ever hear anything like that come out of a clarinet before? I mean, fantastic.

Leslie: [*To* **Horncastle**] Got a quid?

Horncastle: [*Feeling in his pocket*] Gin and bloody lime. What happened to the girl from the petrol pump?

Leslie: [*To the* **barmaid**] Not much lime, love. [*To* **Horncastle**] I'm socially mobile, upwards.

Horncastle: You stay in your class, boy, believe me. Middle-class girls are frigid, you know. They concrete them up till they're married.

Leslie: I think she has a certain style.

Horncastle: To me they all look as if they just got off a horse. Or a cello. Gin and bloody lime, you can't afford that.

Leslie: We'll wean her on to beer. [*To the* **barmaid**] Got a tray, love?

Cut to: the band playing its next number. We see **Monica**'s *hand* *sliding into* **Leslie**'s. *He squeezes her hand. Then* **Monica** *withdraws it.* **Leslie** *opens his hand: there are two pound notes in it.*

Monica: I work for a living.
Leslie: I couldn't.
Enthusiast: [*From behind*] Belt up, mate.
Leslie: [*Low*] It's wrong.
Monica: [*Low*] Look, I'm going to drink lots more gin and lime.
Leslie: [*Low*] Well, all right then.
Monica: [*Holding up her glass*] Hooray. Cheers.

Enthusiast *taps* **Leslie** *on the head with his fist.* **Leslie** *turns angrily.* **Monica** *laughs.*

23 The street outside the pub (1956)
People are coming out into the street from the jazz concert. The Council House clock in the background chimes 10.30.

Horncastle: Great, I thought. Bloody marvellous.
Forcett: A compelling valid spontaneity.
Dora: Why don't you all come back for coffee?
Monica: I have to get up early.
Horncastle: But we haven't *discussed* it, yet.
Forcett: And if it isn't discussed, it hasn't happened.
Leslie: [*As he turns we see he has a black eye. To* **Monica**] The night's yet young.
Monica: Well, I'm not a discussion fiend, but why not? Let's go.

The group walk along the street, **Leslie** *taking* **Monica**'s *hand. The council clock face shines over the roofs.*

24 Horncastle's bedsitter, Nottingham (1956)
The bedsitter is a biggish room in a Victorian or Georgian house in the park. A double bed is against the wall, dressed as a couch. There is a period record player and many records, including many 78s. There are also Penguin Books about, a cactus and Chianti

bottle table lamp. The group is sitting around on chairs or cushions on the floor. **Dora** *putting a shilling in the meter.*

Monica: What I don't understand is, why does everybody have to get onto everybody about class? I mean, I'm a person, you're a person, that's all that's necessary.

Horncastle: But you don't talk like what we do. You don't think like what we do. Class hasn't gone, kid, it's right here.

Dora [*Putting on an apron*] Coffee for everyone? Is bottled all right?

Forcett: Camp, my dears.

Horncastle: It's become the British substitute for sex. You replace a real distinction with an artificial one.

Forcett: Very sensible. Sex you can get anywhere in the world. But class, I mean, real class, you can only get in Britain.

Horncastle: Exactly. Part of the national fantasy. God made the British first.

Forcett: And how right He was.

Horncastle: But we can't go on thinking like that. It's not 1910, the sun doesn't keep on shining on the British Empire, there isn't even much of it to rain on:

Monica: I don't see what that's got to do with me having a gin and lime. I mean, I just like gin and lime.

Horncastle: I've nothing against gin and lime. I've nothing against cavalry twill trousers and tweeds. I've nothing against girls who say 'Golly gosh'. I just say it's part of our deep-seated avoidance of contemporary reality.

Monica: I don't like beer. I don't like the taste.

Leslie: What would you put in its place?

Horncastle: Well, I'd put sex back in its rightful position.

Forcett: Which position do you recommend?

Horncastle: What I mean is, if Freud hadn't mentioned it, I don't think the British would even have noticed. One has this terrible fear of undressing an Englishwoman and finding nothing there at all.

Dora: [*With the coffee*] Oh, really?

Horncastle: This is why jazz matters. It's the real feeling. The line of the emotion. Work music, street tart's songs, the sound of suffering humanity. [*He gets up and goes to the record player*] Let me play you something? I've got everything. Monica?

Monica: Oh. I'll let Leslie choose for me.

Leslie: She'd like something quiet. Chico Hamilton.

Horncastle: [*Putting on a record*] Well, there we go, everything in stock.

The record begins.

Leslie: Oh, Christ. My last bus. I've got to go home.

Horncastle: His daddy'll be cross if he's late.

Leslie: [*To* **Monica**] Walk you home?

Monica rises, baffled.

Monica: It's all right. I can find my way.

Leslie: No. I'll see you back.

25 Some steps into a park, Nottingham (1956)

Monica and Leslie are coming down the steps.

Leslie: He's right, of course.

Monica: Is he? He doesn't like me.

Leslie: He's wrong then.

Monica: I offend him. My class. Do I offend you?

Leslie: I think you're just like the rest of us.

26 A Nottingham street (1956)

Leslie and Monica are outside her flat in the park.

Monica: That was very nice.

Leslie: Yes. [*He kisses her*]

Monica: Uuummm. Your last bus.

Leslie: I'll see you again?

Monica: If you like.

Leslie: Arboretum, same time tomorrow?

Monica: Yes.

Leslie: Hey. [*He kisses her again, then turns and begins running full speed down the slope*] Night!

27 Castle Boulevard, Nottingham (1956)

A lighted bus approaches. The Council House clock strikes eleven fifteen. **Leslie** *runs full speed out of the park, towards the bus. He waves at it. It seems it won't stop. It does.* **Leslie** *gets on.*

28 A teaching room, Shakespeare Street (1956)

From a rather ancient record player, though of postwar vintage, comes the sound of Dylan Thomas reading from his 'Do not go gentle into that good night'. As the poem goes on, we see the evening class gathered together. **Leslie** *is at the head of the table, as the tutor. The group around the table is rather small:* **Leslie** *is not actually one of the world's biggest teaching lures. The group consists of:* **the knitting lady**, *middle-aged and comfortable, knitting throughout;* **Mrs Bone**, *a lady not happy with her husband;* **the thin nun***;* **the man of the people**, *in his shirtsleeves;* **Horncastle***;* **Dora Horncastle***;* **Forcett***;* **Monica**. **Leslie** *suddenly takes the needle off the record, from the player which is placed beside him.*

Leslie: There you are, the poet himself reading it. Now I asked you to look it over at home last week, from the set book, didn't I?

Knitting lady: Yes, you did, Mr Potter.

Leslie: And come with a prepared and adequate critical response. Criticism: the common pursuit of true judgement.

Knitting lady: Yes, that's what you said, Mr Potter.

Leslie: Well, what did you think?

Knitting lady: I thought it rattled along quite marvellously.

Forcett: [*Faint in background*] Rattled along quite marvellously!

Leslie: I see. [*To* **Mrs Bone**] What did you think, Mrs Bone?

Mrs Bone: I must say I found it extremely sensuous. As someone who has not been exactly happy in emotional matters, well, moving, I found, most moving.

Leslie: Sister Mary Magdalene?

Nun: Is Mr Thomas Christian?

Forcett: Excuse me, if I can introduce a caveat, isn't biographical information really irrelevant to a critical assessment? I mean, shouldn't we look at the text in and for itself?

Leslie: I think Mr Forcett's absolutely right. [*To the* **Nun**] Are there any grounds for reading it *as* a Christian poem?

Nun: I couldn't find any faith in it. Of course all can be grist to the divine mill, in a sense.

Leslie: But hardly a devotional poem, a poem of faith.

Nun: Oh, no, not a poem of faith.

Leslie: We don't seem to be getting near a reading. Would you regard it as a mature poem?

Nun: Mr Potter, you use the word 'mature' a lot. What would you say it means?

Leslie: It means an open affirming attitude towards life. Mr Biffin?

Man of the people: [*Scratching his back in thought*] Well, they amuse me, this lot, they do really. I mean, it's about the repression of the bourgeoisie, innit?

Leslie: The repression of the bourgeoisie?

Man of the people: Well, I mean it's about fighting back, innit? And it's about sex, innit? About not repressing, I'd say. About the waste of virginity.

Leslie: Well, perhaps we're getting a bit nearer. An attack on repression. Perhaps even a political poem. But what about the technique and tone of the poem? Miss Dobbs?

Monica *looks up from her furtive reading of a magazine.*

Monica: I'm sorry, I wasn't listening too carefully.
Leslie: The tone and technique of the poem.

Monica *holds a quick whispered conference with* **Forcett** *who is next to her.*

Monica: We think it's a lyrical celebration of Freudian values in a neo-surrealistic mode.
Leslie: You do?

29 Monica's bedsitter (1956)

*Like the Horncastles', **Monica**'s bedsitter is in a high-ceilinged large-ish room in an old house. There are similar fifties' motifs: cacti, paperbacks, etc. The kitchen end has a cooker, a single bed with a cover to make a couch. There is sitting space round a gas fire: Two armchairs.*

Monica: Like some coffee?
Leslie: [*Seeing to the meter*] Bottled?
Monica: Real. Or is that bourgeois?
Leslie: No. Just reading *Horse and Hound* in my class.
Monica: You know, Leslie, I'm not intellectual. I'm very simple and conventional. I suppose, to you, stupid. Nice for a while, but stupid.
Leslie: You're not . . . You like to pretend to be. You're just . . . stable.
Monica: And you're intense. You teach, you write, you want to do something. That's fine, but I'm not like that.

Leslie *gets up from the fire and looks around.*

Leslie: You run all this single-handed?

Monica: Well, two-handed. It's not much.

Leslie: That's good.

Monica: You're praising me for my dusting.

Leslie: [*Finding, above the bed, a soft toy rabbit*] What's this?

Monica: Denzil. A boyfriend gave him to me. I'm afraid it's not very mature.

Leslie: You cook for yourself?

Monica: That's utterly ordinary. Most people do.

Leslie: But work all day too. Lots of boyfriends?

Monica: Some.

Leslie: Go out a lot?

Monica: Yes. What about you?

Leslie: Girlfriends? The word's not right. I believe in serious dealings, you know, not the mating game.

Monica: You do?

Leslie: I don't mean getting engaged, married, that sort of thing. That's the game too. I mean, intelligent, deep relationships. I think men and women can have them, don't you?

Monica: What's wrong with getting engaged?

Leslie: You end up married.

Monica: Isn't that the best thing to do if people love each other?

Leslie: Well, it's a commercial property contract, isn't it?

Monica: It's a Christian ceremony.

Leslie: But you can't contract for love.

Monica: If these people with intelligent, deep relationships want to have these relationships for the rest of their lives, how do they do it?

Leslie   They just do it. Live together.

Monica: Fine for the man. If she gets left holding the baby? What then?

Leslie: If there's nothing left, there's nothing left.

Monica *sees to the coffee.* **Leslie** *comes up behind her and puts his hands round her waist.*

Leslie: Hey. Turn round.

Monica *turns. He kisses her face. A pause, then she responds.*

Monica: You picked me up.
Leslie: You meet people that way.
Leslie: We're not so different. You're mature.
Monica: Mr Potter, you use the word 'mature' a
  lot.
Leslie: Look, come on the bed.
Monica: [*Shaking her head*] Uh-huh. Like this.
Leslie: It's easier lying down.
Monica: I know what's easier lying down.

Pause

Leslie: Did you read the Freud?
Monica: No. *Horse and Hound*.
Leslie: You don't understand your sexual nature.
Monica: Let me see to the coffee.
Leslie: You read it.
Monica: Leslie, I'll come out with you if you want me
  to. I'd like to. But please don't set me homework.
  All right?

Leslie *says nothing.*

30 A trendy boutique in Birmingham (1976)
The boutique is busy. Rock music blares from loudspeakers. Girls select dresses from the racks and take them to the changing room to try on. **Monica**, *holding three dresses on hangers, stands in front of* **Leslie**.

Monica: Which do *you* like best?
Leslie: They're not wildly exciting.
Monica: You mean the neckline doesn't come down
  to my crotch.

103

She goes towards the fitting room.

31 The arboretum (1956)

Leslie *and* **Monica** *are lying wrapped around each other on the grass. There are picnic remnants around them. We hear murmurs from within the human bundle.*

Monica: We're in the middle of a park.
Leslie: Lawrence says it's best outside.
Monica: Lawrence never seemed to get ants in his pants, like everybody else.

On the edge of the shot, a **park keeper**'s *spiked stick appears. It stabs and collects a wrapper from the picnic. The* **park keeper** *stands over them.* **Leslie** *and* **Monica** *sit up suddenly. The* **park keeper** *points to the rubbish.* **Leslie** *picks it up and puts it back in their basket.*

32 The boutique (1976)

Monica *comes out of the changing room in one of the more stuffy dresses.* **Leslie** *sits in a chair in the boutique, shaking his head.* **Monica** *goes back.* **Leslie** *looks at another* **girl** *trying on a dress.*

33 A boating lake at the university (1956)

A long shot across the lake. **Leslie** *and* **Monica** *in a rowing boat. It is just about to disappear out of sight behind an island.*

Leslie: You're really highly sexed.
Monica: Am I?
Leslie: Of course you are. It's nothing to do with class. Middle-class girls do it the same as other girls.
Monica: You've done it with other girls?
Leslie: Yes, of course.
Monica: Lots of girls?
Leslie: Quite a lot. Three.
Monica: Do I know them?
Leslie: How would you know them?
Monica: It must be terrible first time. For the girl.

Leslie: It's not.

Monica: I'd hate myself.

Leslie: You'd love yourself much more.

34 The boutique (1976)

Monica *comes out of the changing room in an unappropriate dress.*

   Leslie, *indifferent to her, is talking to the* **shop girl**.

35 Monica's bedsitter (1956)

The dialogue starts over the end of the previous scene.

Leslie: [*Out of vision*] Let me undo it.

A twang of elastic.

Monica: [*Out of vision*] Hey, that's my suspender belt.

Now we see the room. It is almost dark, but there is a table lamp on. **Monica** *and* **Leslie** *are shadowy figures on the bed.*

Leslie: Hey, I'm falling off.

There is a knocking on the door.

Voice outside: Miss Dobbs, dear? Have you a shilling for the meter?

Silence.

Voice outside: Miss Dobbs? I saw you come in.

Monica: Quick, find my bra.

36 A supermarket (1976)

It is afternoon. We hear taped contemporary music and announcements of bargains.

   Leslie *and* **Monica** *are walking down an aisle, both pushing carts.*

Monica: Mango chutney. Uncle Charles likes that.

She takes three and throws them in the cart. They move on, turn the corner and confront a large stack of toilet rolls at the end of the aisle on special offer.

Monica: Leslie, get two dozen of those.
Leslie: Just what is your uncle coming here to do?

Cut to **Leslie** *with his cart at the checkout counter. There is little in it but the two dozen toilet rolls. He begins unloading the rolls for the* **cashier***.*

Fay: [*Out of the shot*] Did the scampi upset your stomach?

Leslie turns. **Fay** *is standing next in line behind him, carrying an armful of shopping.*

Leslie: Fay. Bulk buying. Monica.

Fay *turns to look as* **Monica** *comes up behind her.*
   The three of them stand in line at the checkout.

37 A Nottingham pub: Trip to Jerusalem (1956)
Monica *and* **Leslie** *sit at a table with drinks.* **Monica** *is drinking beer. The table is largeish: they are waiting for others.* **Monica** *is building a house with the beer mats.*

Leslie: You ought to read it. I'm sure there's authentic genius.
Monica: [*Dull*] Did you say Beckett by Murphy or Murphy by Beckett? Leslie?
Leslie: Yes.
Monica: Do you ever feel differently about things?
Leslie: Monica. They let off a hydrogen bomb. There's a cold war. Who can think of permanent ties? If two people have a mature relationship . . .
Monica: It's not a sodding mature relationship, if you want to know. I don't want to tie you down, I don't want to ruin your sodding talent, I want to be with you, that's all. I'm always with you, it's going nowhere, you're always at my pants, I'm feeling ill.

Leslie: Let's live together.

Monica: Where and on what? What would my father say? What would *your* father say?

Leslie: The killing power of convention.

Monica: Yes. The power of it. If we lived in London, but no, you don't like London. You've got roots. In the great provincial reality. You want to look at the reality. It's your aunts, your dad, your friends, your, what is it, thirty bob a week, just enough for the beer and the Beckett.

Forcett *and* **Dora** *are standing by the table.*

Forcett: You may be three drinks ahead, but you missed a very fine lecture on Sartrean existentialism. Didn't they, Dora?

Monica: It's also me. I'm not bloody Freida Lawrence. I don't read Jung and throw plates.

Leslie: I know. Where's Dennis?

Dora: [*Sitting down*] Getting some drinks.

Monica: I'll leave you to cultivate your avant garden. [*Knocking down the card house and getting up*]

Monica *goes.* **Horncastle**, *holding a tray of drinks, starts after her.*

Horncastle: I've bought her a drink.

Dora: [*Arm round* **Leslie**] Leslie's upset. Poor old Les.

Horncastle: [*Sitting down*] Don't go, Leslie, you'll lose your outsider status. What would Colin Wilson say?

Forcett: Sartre? Camus?

38 A shopping precinct car park (1976)

In the car park, **Leslie** *and* **Monica** *are carrying large loads of parcels and a hat stand to the car.*

Leslie, *unloading the parcels into the boot, is trying to arrange the hat stand on the car.*

Monica: Who was that in the supermarket?
Leslie: Oh, someone at work.

39 Monica's bedsitter (1956)
Monica *is in a dressing gown in front of the fire.* **Leslie** *is in shirt and trousers.*
Monica: No?
Leslie: No. I hadn't got any. I thought you never would.
Monica: But you had some before.
Leslie: I gave them to Forcett. I thought you weren't going to.
Monica: You used them. You used them.
Leslie: [*The Council House clock chimes*] Christ. The last bus.
Monica: Oh, God.
Leslie: It's a four-mile walk if I miss it.
Monica: Stay here.
Leslie: [*Pulling on his jacket*] I've got to go. [*Pause*] I have to rush.

Monica *looks at him.*

Leslie: I'll have to run like hell. Night, Monica [*Kisses her head*] Tomorrow. I'll come here.

Monica *looks at him.*

40 A street (1956)
Leslie *is sprinting towards Castle Boulevard.*

41 Castle Boulevard (1956)
The lighted bus comes slowly along. **Leslie** *runs madly out of the park. The bus passes the stop. He races across the road, just too late. He waves his fist after the bus. The bus stops.*

Conductor: Come on then, surrey.

Leslie *runs to get on the bus.*

42 The top deck of the bus (1956)
Leslie *sits panting in an upstairs seat. The* **conductor** *stands beside him.*

Conductor: Oo, you'll kipper yourself, you will. You get some exercise, don't you?
Leslie: [*Panting*] Yes.
Conductor: Fourth night this week.
Leslie: Yes.
Conductor: What have you got up there, whippets?
Leslie: Girl.
Conductor: We ought to drive round to her front door. Save you all this puff and blow.
Leslie: Am I the only one on?
Conductor: We run this for you. You're on to a good thing. Own driver, two hundred horsepower purring smoothly under the bonnet . . .
Leslie: What do you do if a girl gets pregnant?
Conductor: I'd run, mate. Twice as fast as yo' come down that hill.

43 Outside the Potters' house, Solihull (1976)
The MGB, with the hat stand precariously balanced on it, turns into the drive of the modern, contemporary executive style house in a wooded avenue. It parks in front of the garage. Three **children** *are sitting hopelessly on the doorstep.*

44 The hall/kitchen of a council house (1956)
This is a prewar council house in fringe Nottingham, University side.

The door opens and **Leslie** *comes in with his shoes in his hand. He tiptoes towards the kitchen. In the kitchen, he looks in the cabinets, finds a bottle of milk and a glass. He pours himself a drink, sits down at the kitchen table, stares blankly.*

Mr Potter: What time do you call this?

Mr Potter *is standing in the kitchen doorway, in pyjamas and an old thick wool dressing gown.*

Leslie: Oh, hello, dad. I don't know, what is it? Half past ten?

Mr Potter: Don't talk daft, it's nearly midnight. You were on that last bus again.

Leslie: Can it be?

Mr Potter: If you come on that again, they'll be spitting on your photograph down the garage. What do you do at this hour? Everything's shut.

Leslie: I talk to my friends. Discuss matters.

Mr Potter: Never a thought for your mother. You know she can't sleep when you're not in.

Leslie: Why not? I can sleep when she's not in.

Mr Potter: Watch it. Your mother's never not in. Especially at this time.

Leslie: People do customarily go out in the evenings. All over the world.

Mr Potter: You'll know what I'm talking about one day. When you've kids of your own. I'd like to see the day, that's all. My God. It's time you were on your own, it is, with a family.

Leslie: Can you be on your own *and* have a family?

Mr Potter: Don't come here with that smart university talk. It may impress your friends in pubs. It doesn't me. I don't know what that university's done to you.

Leslie: Made me an intelligent, critical human being.

Mr Potter: It's made you bone idle. You do nowt all day, you've got all these daft ideas. It's paradise, for some. And we're the poor fools who are expected to run an all night cafe for you whenever you feel like a bit of roof over your head.

Leslie: I'm a thinker, dad.

Mr Potter: Your mother said this night: all he's here
          for is to get his socks washed. That's all we see of
          you. A pile of dirty socks. I'd just like to see you lift
          a finger for once.

Leslie: In what particular gesture?

Mr Potter: That does it. Get off to bed. [**Leslie** *gets up*]
          And don't make a row flushing that thing, either,
          and waking your mother.

Leslie: You said she was . . .

Mr Potter: Go on. Upstairs.

45 The hall of the Potters' house (1976)

Leslie *pushes open the front door and comes in, laden with
bundles of shopping.* **Monica** *is in the hall, attending to the three*
children*, who are taking off coats, etc.*

Leslie: [*Putting down his burdens*] Didn't they know we
          were going shopping?

Monica: Yes, of course they did. But Jason wouldn't
          go to the school youth club. He says it was full of
          youths.

Leslie: What a shock, Jason. How did *they* get there?

The **child** *is crying again.*

Monica: [*To* **children**] I want you all to go upstairs
          and change into your playclothes. Daddy's tired.

Leslie: You can tell by his sarcasm.

The **children** *go upstairs.*

Monica: You could be nicer, couldn't you, they
          haven't seen you all day. [*She sees where* **Leslie** *has
          put the shopping*] Oh, Leslie, not there, please. I am
          trying against all the odds to keep the house reason-
          ably tidy. Elaine Montefiore's coming in to see me
          about her divorce.

Leslie: I always think one of the great advantages of

divorce is the number of people it lets you discuss
your sex life with.

Monica: It's not funny, Leslie. I know you think I
shouldn't interfere. But people can talk to me.

Leslie: Hmm.

46 The teaching room, Shakespeare Street (1956)

*The vintage record player: on it, a record of E. E. Cummings
reading 'Anyone Lived in a Pretty How Town'.*

Anyone lived in a pretty how town
(with up so floating many bells down)
spring summer autumn winter
he sang his didn't he danced his did.

Women and men (both little and small)
cared for anyone not at all
they sowed their isn't they reaped their same
sun moon stars rain.

*During this we pan round the room. We gradually see the class. It
is summer: the group is in seasonable clothes. The **nun** is not
present this time, but we see the **man of the people**, laughing
appreciatively, nudging **Mrs Bone** who is fanning herself in the
heat; the **knitting lady**, her needles bouncing up and down to
the rhythm: **Horncastle** and **Dora Horncastle**; and **Forcett**,
expressing distaste. Finally, we see **Monica**'s empty place.
Leslie is looking at it. He takes off the needle.*

47 Horncastle, Dora, Forcett, Leslie are sitting outside a Nottingham pub (1956)

Horncastle: Oh, Leslie. No.

Dora: Leslie, what have you been doing?

Horncastle: It's bloody obvious what he's been doing.
Of course if he only went and got his hair cut, he'd
know what they have at the barbers.

Forcett: Has she asked you to . . .?

Leslie: No, she hasn't. I think she's trying not to.

Horncastle: Well, if she does, don't.

Forcett: Women. If they could only find a safe way of defusing them, they'd be the most marvellous invention in the world.

Horncastle: It'll come.

Leslie: I should have waited, shouldn't I?

Horncastle: Now listen, I know you. I know your ethic of concern. But there are all sorts of things you can do besides getting married.

Leslie: Don't worry, Horncastle. I won't.

Horncastle: I've got some money, you've got friends, boy. I'll buy you a drink right away . . .

48 The Potters' sitting room (1976)

Monica, **Elaine**, **Montefiore** and **Leslie** *are talking.*

Elaine: If I could just take that bit of me off and put it in the spare room for him to have a go at, I'm sure we'd both be perfect partners.

Monica: He doesn't see you as a person?

Elaine: I'm not sure what a person is. But it's object status. That's what my gestalt therapist says.

Monica: Look, did you think of getting this therapist to talk to Hugh?

Elaine: Well, there's a complication there. Hugh knows I went to bed with him. I thought it would be clever to tell him.

Monica: I thought you'd . . .

Elaine: Kept my nose clean? I didn't tell you that bit. This is what Hugh can't get. How I'm off it with him and on it with Zachery.

Leslie: It takes imagination.

Elaine: The point is, it's not the same. With Zachery it's something else, not physical.

Leslie: That's quite a discovery. Do you use pollen?

Elaine: Leslie, you know what I mean. It's psychological. With him, I'm whole, I realize myself.

113

Monica: You're in love with him?

Elaine: Zachery? Well, no. I mean, he's twice married, he probably does it with all his patients. But he doesn't type me in a role. I start again with him.

Monica: But you want to go to him.

Elaine: No. If it wasn't for Hugh, there wouldn't be Zachery, if you see what I mean. It's a sort of necessary pair. Like bookends.

Monica: I don't understand really. No.

Leslie: What about Hugh? Has he got someone else?

Elaine: Well, you know Hugh. He's probably having it off with half the crescent. Has he been here?

Monica: I don't think he'd get far with me, do you?

Elaine: Oh, I know, he wouldn't try. I mean to talk about it.

Leslie: Oh, is he talking too?

Elaine: That's what we do. [*Turning to* **Leslie**] It's like a bloody trade union negotiation. We try conciliation, but we've taken our positions, and there we stick. Anyway, are we going?

Monica: Oh, I didn't . . .

Elaine: Haven't you told Leslie?

Leslie: What is there to tell?

Elaine: There's a new encounter group starting in the church hall tonight. Hugh and I are going, we thought we ought to try. But we wanted you to come.

Leslie: I don't want to go to an encounter group. I spend all my time avoiding encounters.

Elaine: That's why you need to go.

49 The teaching room, Shakespeare Street (1956)

The class, again in summer clothes. It is very hot. Auden's poem 'One Evening' is heard from the record player.

Plunge your hands in the water
Plunge them in up to the wrist;

Stare, stare in the basin
And wonder what you've missed.

The glacier knocks in the cupboard,
The desert sighs in the bed,
And the crack in the teacup opens
A land to the land of the dead

Where the beggars raffle the banknotes . . .

We see that **Monica** *is back again.*

50 Beside the river Trent (1956)
It is evening.

Monica: Did you think you were going to have to
marry me?
Leslie: No.
Monica: No?
Leslie: I wasn't going to be forced into it.
Monica: You'd have left me to it?
Leslie: Look, Monica; will you now?
Monica: What?
Leslie: Marry me.

Pause.

Monica: That's ridiculous.
Leslie: Why is it ridiculous? I want to.
Monica: You don't have to any more.
Leslie: I never had to.
Monica: Why now and not then?
Leslie: I'm freely choosing.
Monica: Why do you want to? You don't believe in it.
Leslie: That night when we did, and I left you. You
looked so sad. I decided you were real.
Monica: I've always been real.
Leslie: I had to feel it. Look, will you think about it?
Just think about it.

Monica: You said it was a bourgeois institution.

Leslie: It is, of course. I'm proposing reform from within.

Monica: You think we can?

Leslie: We're going into it seriously. Not just because it's done. Aren't we?

Monica: Yes.

Leslie: Marriage is a changing institution. Every generation makes it afresh. Like the law. Oh, wait till I tell Horncastle. He'll never forgive me.

Monica: You're not doing it to be kind.

Leslie: I'm not kind.

51 The Potters' dining room (1976)

Supper is being taken.

Leslie: Elaine's been leaving Hugh for five years. Her divorce is an essential part of her marriage.

Monica: I know, they're just bourgeois people. But they do have bad times too.

Leslie: Yes.

Slight pause.

Monica: You don't think it might do some good.

Leslie: What?

Monica: Going to this group.

Leslie: No. I don't fancy the bourgeois cures. Everybody we know sees somebody. Somebody sees everybody. Is anybody any different? This is not quite where I wanted to end up.

Monica: No, you meant to stay twenty for ever, but we couldn't fix it. You know, I actually would like you to be happy, believe it or not. It would be nice even for me. Remember me?

Leslie: Yes, I do.

52 Inside Nottingham University library (1956)

Horncastle: No, you're not.

Leslie: I am.

Forcett: Leslie, you're not.

Leslie: Really.

Horncastle: It's a bloody disaster.

Librarian: Shush!

53 The university campus (1956)

Horncastle, **Forcett** and **Leslie** *are sitting on the grass.*

Leslie: But you're married!

Horncastle: But I've never written anything.

Forcett: There's only one good rule for a writer. If you must marry, if, marry a wealthy woman who admires your work profoundly.

Horncastle: Preferably more profoundly than you do.

Forcett: Who'll keep you. Writing won't keep you. If a writer makes money, a good writer, he makes it when he's dead. Widows sometimes benefit.

Horncastle: Is she going to keep you?

Leslie: No. She wants to stop work.

Horncastle: Oh, God, Leslie.

Forcett: You don't know when you're lucky. Look at you. The state supports you while you write . . .

Horncastle: You live the independent life of the mind. With brilliant, stimulating companions. And Forcett.

Forcett: You know I don't give critical praise lightly. But those two opening chapters of yours, they're, well, little short of brilliant. That's a judicious critical estimate. Measuring against the great norms. Lawrence, George Eliot, the Dickens of *Hard Times*.

Leslie: Oh, I think that overstates it a bit.

Horncastle: She drinks gin and lime. She likes children, she'll have dozens. She belongs to tennis clubs. Those clothes don't come from Marks and Sparks, Leslie, Leslie, you'll end up in work.

Leslie: I've thought about that. I'll go on writing. I'll continue part-time with the thesis. I'll get a related job. Teaching.

Horncastle: You need a diploma.

Leslie: Copywriting.

Forcett: It's a betrayal. A misuse of the tool of language which the writer has a duty to keep clean.

Leslie: She believes in me as a writer. She'll help me.

Horncastle: She has the critical instincts of a pork butcher. You think it's all so bloody mature. It's a sellout.

Leslie: I've never touched real life. Ordinary experience. I've never felt through the guts.

Forcett: It's bloody Lawrence that's done this.

Horncastle: The whole point of marriage is to stop you getting anywhere near real life. You think it's a great struggle with the mystery of being. It's more like . . . being smothered in warm cocoa. There's sex, but it's not what you think. Marvellous, for the first fortnight. Then every Wednesday. If there isn't a good late-night concert on the Third. Meanwhile you become a biological functionary. An agent of the great female womb, spawning away, dumping its goods in your lap for succour. Daddy, daddy, We're here, and we're expensive.

Forcett: [*Holding up the paper*] This is the real life, Leslie. Kicking the British nationals out of Egypt. For the first time things are hotting up politically in this country.

Horncastle: And when the call comes, where will you be. Under the cocoa.

Leslie: Look, I'm not opting *out*. I want a real relationship. Arthur Miller's marrying Marilyn Monroe. Why shouldn't I marry Monica Dobbs?

Forcett: He's bloody going to.

Horncastle: I give it six months. When?

118

Leslie:　When her brother gets leave from Cyprus. October, it looks like. He's giving her away.

Horncastle:　At least you're lucky he's not going to charge.

Leslie:　Dennis. I wondered if you'd be best man.

Pause.

Horncastle:　All right, Leslie. Not best, perhaps, but as good as I can be.

54 A church hall in Birmingham (1976)

The encounter group sits around on less than comfortable chairs.
*The **group leader**, also in the circle, is probably American.*
*The group consists of **Monica** and **Leslie** (together),*
Elaine *and* **her husband** *and four or five others.*

Group leader:　Okay, there's something wrong in society, and it makes us wrong. You know it, that's why you've come. What is it? Society gives us roles and masks, we live behind them, we never get out. We don't see other people, know them, feel them. And we don't feel ourselves. Isn't that the problem?

Some murmurs.

Group leader:　You don't even answer me, you will. You're all new to this experience?

Murmurs of 'yes'.

Group leader:　All right, you're afraid, you're wondering whether you should have chosen car-maintenance. Maybe you've come hoping to feel up a pretty girl or boy. It's not about that. You won't know for a bit what it is like. It's about getting beyond fear, revealing ourselves, reaching the person. Now all you're going to do, all you're going to do for the next few minutes, is say three words. Awareness.

Intimacy. Spontaneity. Right? Awareness. Intimacy. Spontaneity. Okay, go ahead.

Group: [*Hesitant*] Awareness. Intimacy. Spontaneity.

Group leader: Aware-ness. Intimacy. Spontan-eity.

Group: Awareness. Intimacy. Spontaneity. Awareness. Intimacy . . .

Group leader: Now stand up and move while you're
saying it.

Group: [*Doing so*] Spontaneity. Awareness. Intimacy
. . .

55 The living room of a council house, Nottingham (1956)

*We see Sir Anthony Eden on the screen in black and white. He is
making his Suez speech in which he speaks of 'our quarrel with
Colonel Nasser . . . who cannot be trusted'. Gradually we see the
picture is on a black and white set of the period.*

Mr *and* **Mrs Potter** *are watching the speech, with mugs of
tea.* **Leslie** *comes in. He wears a smart suit and has had a haircut.*

Mr Potter: That's our lifeline to the world. If he
doesn't do something about it, this country's
finished. We'll be a daft, cissy country with no
point, won't we? [*Pause*] You'll be fighting in this
before you've done.

Mrs Potter: What about his cough?

Leslie: On which side did you see me?

Mr Potter: Our bloody side. It'll be against the
Russians before we've done.

Mrs Potter: I thought the Russians were all right now.

Mr Potter: They're interfering in Hungary now. They
don't change their spots, you know. I tell you, this is
the only place in the world where there's a decent
life, and how long will that last?

Mrs Potter: What this country needs is Winnie back.

Leslie: [*Sitting looking at screen*] Is that Winnie the
Churchill or Winnie the Pooh?

Pause

Mr Potter: Apologize to your mother.
Leslie: I'm sorry, mother.

56 The church hall (1976)

Group leader: You're saying that from your heads.
They're up here and under them are your bodies,
right? Now, do you know what stops those bodies
saying anything? You ever hear of muscular
armour?

Murmurs.

Group leader: Okay, you didn't. A man called Reich
talked about it. Muscular armour is body protection
arising from tensions. We're going to start un-
plating that armour. Let's begin with some simple
touchwork. That sound fun?

Murmurs, agreement and laughter.

Group leader: It's not all fun, though, wait till you
start seeing each other. Anyone here know anyone
else here? I'm going to have to split them.
Monica and Elaine: [*together*] Yes. We do.
Group leader: You're . . .
Monica: Monica.
Group leader: Okay, Monica. [*To* **Leslie**] And
you're . . .
Leslie: Herbert.
Monica: He's not Herbert.
Group leader: Ah-ha . . .
Group leader: Well, you go right over there, away
from him, Monica. Okay, I'm going to go round and
designate each of you toucher, or touched. Toucher,
touched, toucher, touched, toucher, touched . . .
[*Right round the group*]

Murmurs and rearrangement in group.

Group leader: This is straight barrier-breaking. I want the touchers to reach out and touch the touched, wait a minute, I'm going to tell you just where. [*Laughter*] On the head. [*More laughter*] Early days yet. On the head, touch the head, shut your eyes, feel the head, feel the feel of the head, feel, feel, feel the head until it's really . . . heady. Touched, feel the hand, take it *into* the head, right through into the body behind it.

*A shot of **Leslie**'s face, held and fondled by a large lady.*

57 A hotel room in Nottingham (1956)

Leslie, *in his one smart suit, comes into the room. There are two interviewers*, **Mark** *and* **Paul**.

Paul: Oh, Mr Potter, come in, I'm Paul, this is Mark, please sit there.

Leslie: Thank you.

Paul: Cigarette, Leslie, may I call you Leslie?

Leslie: Please, thank you.

Mark: Smoke a lot, Leslie?

Leslie: No, not much, just in the odd stressful moment.

Paul: [*Lighting the cigarette*] This is a stressful moment?

Leslie: Yes, being interviewed.

Mark: Have a lot of stressful moments?

Leslie: No more than most.

Paul: We know you're not psychotic, we have this psychological test you did. We use an extravert/introvert scale.

Mark: Would you say you were more introvert than extravert, or vice versa? Have a guess.

Leslie: More introvert.

Paul: Right. You have a seventy per cent introversion quotient. So how do you get on with others?

Leslie: I'm greatly interested in people, being a writer.

Mark: We read the piece you sent us. What would you say was the psychology behind that? Would you say you write to fantasize about the relationships you'd like to have, but don't?

Leslie: No.

Paul: Married?

Leslie: I'm getting married. That's why I'm giving up research.

Mark: Wouldn't you put it more positively?

Leslie: Want to work for you.

Paul: Why do you want to work for us?

Leslie: I think working for a vigorous company like yours would be . . . very invigorating.

Paul: Okay, let's talk about soap. Now, do you see soap, detergents, as in any sense a creative contribution to society?

Leslie: Yes. Oh yes.

58 The church hall (1976)

Group leader: This is a game called truth telling. It's not played much. Now I just want you to tell me how you feel. There are some people here you know, some you don't, some you've touched, some you haven't. But we're a group, we're all starting to know everybody. I know it's hard, you don't want to offend, so, okay, I'll start. [*Pause*] I feel, I feel, there's someone here who doesn't want to be here.

Elaine: That's you, Leslie.

Group leader: Okay, I think it's Leslie too. Now how do we know he doesn't want to be here? What game does he play?

Monica: Hard to get.

Group leader: Are you hard to get, Leslie? Do you want to answer?

Leslie: No.

Group leader: Kids play hard to get. Do you think Leslie's being childish?

Elaine: He is, isn't he?

Leslie: No, I'm not. I'm a free chooser, aren't I?

Group leader: But you came. A parent brought you?

Monica: Oh, God, that's me.

Group leader: Ah-ha . . .

59 The hotel room (1956)

Mark: What would you say a person like yourself, high intelligence, creative, could usefully contribute to the production and merchandizing of detergent?

Paul: Or put the question the other way. What could it give you?

Small pause.

Leslie: I've thought about this. I don't see a split between a managerial career and writing. Trollope founded the Post Office. Isn't it, precisely, those qualities of imagination, sympathetic comprehension, moral analysis a writer possesses that mark a good executive? Those gifts would be yours in the day, mine in the evening, sustaining a busy, involved life.

Small pause.

Mark: Rather well said.

Paul: Suppose we mention technical journalism to you.

Mark: We run a house magazine called *Soft Soap*. There's an editorial position.

Leslie: That sounds . . . very interesting.

Paul: Write us a sample story for it. Something related to soap.

Mark: Send it to us in Grimsby.

Paul: If our editors like it, we'd like you to come and be interviewed there.

Mark: Well, thank you, Leslie, for your interest.

Leslie: [*Getting up*] Thank you.

60 The church hall (1976)

Group Leader: I mean, what would be a good name for Leslie? Would you call him a Sulk?

Elaine: He's nice.

Leslie: I think that's irrelevant.

Group Leader: We're all nice. But what relationships have we learned to transact? Family relationships in the culture? I just am asking what Leslie transacts. He's here, he doesn't want to be here, he says, 'Look what they made me do.' I mean, Leslie, do you want to talk about it? Do you often say, look what they made me do?

Monica: Yes, he does.

Group Leader: Oh, Monica, baby, you're in this too. Let him talk, if he'll talk.

Leslie: I suggest we pass to someone else.

Elaine: I think Leslie should talk . . .

61 In Monica's bedsitter. Day. (1956)

The radio is on, with news about the Suez alert. **Monica** *is unpacking wedding presents, and has just unwrapped a Teasmade. She looks rather strained and unhappy.*

   Leslie *in the doorway in his interview suit.*

Monica: Leslie, a suit!

Leslie: Yes, well, I just had the interview.

Monica: How did it go?

Leslie: I'll probably get it. I was pretty persuasive. A job in technical journalism.

Monica: [*In tears, holding him*] Oh, Leslie.

Leslie: I don't mind, Monica, people have to do these things. Mind the suit, I need it for the wedding.

Monica: It's Brian. He can't come. His regiment's on alert. He says there'll be a war. That there's a will to a war.

Leslie: There won't be a war.

Monica: Do you remember the last one?

Leslie: Of course. They bombed me. I was strategic. Five but very clever.

Monica: The men were all called up. They'll take you.

Leslie: They won't take me, I was 4F for National Service. The disabling cough. Anyway, it's all bluster. The last try at British greatness. The fact is, we haven't got the gunboats to send. Anyway, this generation would rise in protest against it.

Monica: Would you?

Leslie: Well, of course. Get out there on the streets.

Monica: But you couldn't. If it was right.

Leslie: How could it be right?

Monica: If the government said it was right.

Leslie: If the government said it was right, they'd be wrong.

Monica: Wouldn't that be treachery?

Leslie: Monica, just lately I've become a small expert in treachery. Horncastle tells me all this is treachery: stopping writing, getting this job, if I've got it, joining the marital club. So no lessons in treachery, eh?

Monica: [*Silence*]

Leslie: I'm just telling you what Horncastle said.

Monica: [*Looks at him*]

62 Newsreel film (October 1956)

We see newsreel film of the build-up towards Suez at the end of October, film of an anti-Suez protest before the invasion, a clip from a condemnation speech, film showing conferences, Eden's illness, and the Hungarian Revolution in Budapest before the entry of the Russians.

63 The wedding reception (October 1956)

In a corner of the room we see **Mr** *and* **Mrs Potter**, *and* **Monica**'s **Uncle** *and* **Horncastle**. *He is in a suit and is standing and making a speech, glass in hand.*

Horncastle: I'm terrible at speeches. This is not a good
day in the world's history. There's still repression of
freedom in Hungary. There's our venture in the
Middle East, I won't go into that.

Mr Potter: No, don't.

Dora: Come on, Dennis, it's a wedding.

Horncastle: Exactly. There's one historical event, a
bit smaller perhaps, but still significant, that ought
to bring the world a modicum of cheer, a touch of
continuity.

Uncle: [*Good accent*] Hear, hear.

Horncastle: Today Leslie Ronald Potter, I didn't
know you were Ronald, Ronald, passing a church
door, fell inside, found himself implicated in a
ceremony, and emerged, a happier man, eh, Ronald,
on the arm of Monica Edwina Dobbs.

Mr Potter: No, no.

Horncastle: I'm sorry. Emerged, I should say, if the
register was signed with real names, as Mr Potter
and Mrs Potter. Ladies and gents, the happy couple.
Here's to them and their future. Now, then, doesn't
he do the reply?

There is some confusion: whose speech is next?

64 Newsreel film (October 1956)

*A glimpse of the anti-Suez demonstration in Trafalgar Square;
troops embark in Cyprus; and crowds in Budapest.*

65 Midland Station, Nottingham (October 1956)

The honeymoon party. **Monica** *is in her going away outfit,*
Leslie *still in his one suit. Also there are* **Mr** *and* **Mrs Potter,**

Monica's **Uncle**, **Horncastle** and **Dora**, *amid the moving crowds going for trains.*

A group photograph is taken: **Mr** *and* **Mrs Potter**, **Monica**, **Monica's Uncle**.

Mrs Potter: It was lovely, Monica. Such a nice reception. Despite the petrol rationing. All ours came.

Monica: Well, thank you, Mrs Potter.

Mr Potter: [*Giving her a kiss*] You're a good girl, you'll look after him.

Monica: Thanks for getting him there on time.

Mr Potter: It's not easy, you know. He'll die in bed, that one.

Mrs Potter: [*Giggling*] This isn't the time to say that, Frank.

Leslie *and* **Horncastle** *are photographed.*

Horncastle: You did it, you did it. And he never looked lovelier, did he?

Dora: [*Standing by*] He looks happy enough.

Horncastle: He should be, he's getting a free holiday at the seaside out of it. If I can find the tickets. [*Feeling in his pockets*] I didn't give them to you instead of the ring?

Leslie: Come on, Dennis. Where's Forcett?

Horncastle: Oh, didn't you know, unavoidably absent. He went to London for the Suez demonstration. See what you're missing? You could have spent tonight in a sleeping bag in Trafalgar Square.

Mr Potter: [*To* **Uncle**] A pity about Brian. Not being able to come.

Mrs Potter: I hope he'll be all right with all this fighting.

Uncle: Likes a bit of adventure. Brian.

Mr Potter: Well, you did sterling service.

Uncle: Passed off all right. Vicar a bit low church, eh?

Horncastle: Here we are, here we are, tickets for two. First class, plush seats.

Mr Potter: First class, for ever, eh?

Mrs Potter [*To* **Uncle**] He's got a very good job. In Grimsby, on a little magazine.

Mr. Potter: [*To everyone*] Can we have just one more snap?

The whole party gets into line, with **Mr Potter** *organizing.*

Horncastle: The train's due in a minute.

Mr Potter: All right then, hold it there. For the record.

The photograph: the shot is frozen and held over the first two speeches of the next scene.

66 The Potters' sitting room (1976)

It is late evening.

Monica: [*Out of vision*] Dennis Horncastle said it wouldn't last.

Leslie: [*Out of vision*] He gave it six months. I've been here for twenty years. That's been me all the time. I'm a monument to constancy.

We now see this scene.

Monica: Is that what you call it? You report home every night. I suppose it's a sort of constancy.

Leslie: People will look back in amazement.

Monica: You have no interest. None in the children, none in me. All right, you work to finance it, or a lot of it. But you leave it to me to lead the life we've made. Then you blame me for it.

Leslie: Did we make it?

Monica: It never had your consent?

Leslie: I think it just happened. The world went that way.

Monica: It didn't just happen. It had to be made, so I made it. I'm an ordinary person, so I made an ordinary life.

Leslie: Not quite ordinary.

Monica: You mean, bourgeois. I'm not particularly proud of it, but it leaves you free to be discontented in comfort. And if you feel it's not your house, not your life, that's because I had to make it. For the last ten years I've been on my own in company.

[*Pause*]

I don't make you happy, do I, Leslie?

Leslie: I'm not a happy person.

Monica: Could you have been?

Leslie: I don't know. Maybe with a bit of life coming my way. A sexuality that wasn't there to feed the biological machine.

Monica: Leslie: this bigger life you're missing, what's her name?

Leslie: Her name?

Monica: I may be simple but I'm not stupid. The comb in the car, the girl in the supermarket. Does she do it right? [*Small pause*] Because if she does, I think you ought to go to her. I mean, I love you, but this house, these kids, this stuff, this flat sex I do, they're really just about my limits.

67 The entrance to the top floor flat (1976)

Leslie *ringing the bell.* **Fay** *comes to the door. She has spectacles on.*

Fay: Oh.

Leslie: Can I talk to you?

Fay: Oh, look, I've got someone here.

Leslie: I see.

130

A **woman** *comes into the hall. Hair in pins, Birmingham accent. She is pulling up her sweater to show her stomach.*

Woman: Look, there's another one. He did that to me for going down the city. We all like a bit of life, don't we?

Leslie: Will you be long?

Fay: She's staying the night. She can't go back there.

Woman: Another down here. He's a great bloody brute, that one.

Fay: I can't talk now. Ring me on Monday.

Leslie: It's all right. [*As he turns to go*] Oh, I brought your comb. You left it in my car.

Fay: Oh, thanks, Leslie.

Leslie: You left it in the car.

Fay: Well, yes. I thought it might make . . . a topic of conversation.

Leslie: It did. Well . . .

Fay: Night.

68 Outside the block of flats (1976)

Leslie *crosses and sits alone in his car. As we watch this scene, we hear the beginning of the next one.*

Monica: Oh, Leslie, that's enough, no more. We'd only just got to sleep.

Leslie: Please.

69 A hotel bedroom (1956)

The English seaside hotel where **Monica** *and* **Leslie** *are spending their honeymoon. They are in bed together: it is early morning.*

Monica: [*Turning over*] Just talk to me.

Leslie: I hope you're not frigid.

Monica: After last night . . .

Leslie: That was last night.

Monica: There's always.

Leslie: Lawrence says . . .

Monica: Lawrence says. Sigmund Freud says. Sex isn't all it's about.

Leslie: What else?

Monica: We'll have to see.

Leslie *gets out of bed. He goes to the window.*

Leslie: Horncastle says it'll last six months.

Monica: Horncastle says. What do you say?

70 Newsreel film (1956)

Film of planes dropping bombs over Cairo and explosions.
    Cut to tanks moving in the desert.
    Cut to a Russian tank moving towards the camera, firing, in the streets of Budapest.

71 The Potters' garden (1976)

Monica *comes out of the house. It is the next day.*

Monica: [*Calling*] Leslie. Can you come and do balsa with Jason?

*We see **Leslie** sitting on a very small tractor lawnmower.*
    A shot from in front of the lawnmower, as if it were an absurd tank. This shot is frozen as the credits roll.

STANDING IN FOR HENRY

Standing in for Henry was first shown on BBC1 in December 1980 in the 'Playhouse' series, with the following cast:

Graham	Simon Nowell-Parker
Verity	Polly Hemingway
Mrs Lips	Brigit Forsyth
Heather	Barbara Flynn
Bruno	Bill Nighy
Martin	Philip Sully
Teddy Finn	Donald Gee
Arthur Ellis	Andrew Bradford
Henry	Christopher Jagger
Designer	Barrie Dobbins
Producer	Rosemary Hill
Director	Michael Heffernan

1 The public house

It is late evening.

Blurred, out of focus images of a crowded bar. There is loud live music. People are dancing.

At a corner table, figures are laughing. Someone comes over with a tray of drinks. The figures in the group, whom we really see only in silhouette, are **Verity**, **Heather**, **Mrs Lips**, **Martin**, *and* **Bruno**. *All are flamboyant people, artists and staff from the art studio round the corner.*

The figure with the drinks – is it **Henry**? *– takes* **Verity** *off on to the floor to dance.*

Cut to **Henry** *dancing with* **Heather**.

Cut to **Henry** *dancing with* **Mrs Lips**.

Over this we see the titles, and then hear the voice of the narrator:

Narrator: Once, in the middle of the sixties, when it was Then and not Now, where there was still Energy to be had, and everyone was into Style, a young man called Graham Peach, who was waiting to go to university . . .

2 A provincial city street

This is one of those streets near the centre of a Midlands provincial city where Georgian houses have been turned over to offices and businesses. Dentists, accountants and solicitors occupy the old living space of the not quite top-class merchants.

Graham Peach *is bicycling precariously down the street – precariously because on the back of his racing bike is strapped a very large art portfolio.* **Graham** *is nineteen, and two worlds show on him – vague Bohemian leanings, modified by the rules of tidiness of his suburban school and home. Thus he wears a school blazer, but has a silk scarf tucked in the neck of an open shirt. His hair is as long as a strict headmaster might allow.*

He cycles towards us, looking from side to side.

Narrator: [*Continuing*] . . . but who really wanted to be an artist (he had been drawing and sketching for years), tried for a summer job in a commercial art studio, to see if this was the life for him.

Cut to a shot of the sign displayed outside one of these houses. It says, in contemporary art work, ELLFINN PUBLICITY.
Graham stops and gets off his bicycle.
Over this, we hear **Mrs Lips** *at her switchboard, out of vision:*

Mrs Lips: Hello, Ellfinn Publicity, best in art and design, can I help you? Oh, Mr Goodrich, yes, right, Mr Goodrich, well, he is in, he's on the phone to *Vogue*, can I give him a, oh, if it's about the Muesli promotion, yes, I'm sure he'll, can you hold, I'll try and connect you. Holding you, Mr Goodrich.

During this, **Graham** *removes the art portfolio, tidies himself, and goes in through the door.*

3 The hall and staircase, Ellfinn Publicity: Graham attends for interview

At the bottom of the stairs a sign says: 'Ellfinn Publicity, Second Floor, please walk up.' **Graham** *looks up and mounts the stairs.*

Mrs Lips: [*Out of vision*] Oh, Mr Finn, sorry to, I've got Mr Goodrich on the line, about the, shall I . . .?

Halfway up the stairs, there is a door marked 'Ellfinn Publicity Only'. **Graham** *pushes it open. He has made a mistake. It is the toilet. On it sits* **Verity**. *She is about twenty-five, dark, beautiful in a pre-Raphaelite style. She stares coolly at him.*

Graham: I'm terribly sorry.
Mrs Lips: [*Out of vision*] Hello, I'm sorry, Mr Goodrich, are you still holding?
Graham: I came about a job.
Verity: Try reception, not the loo. It's upstairs.

Graham: Terribly sorry.

Mrs Lips: [*Out of vision*] Terribly sorry, Mr Finn. Terribly sorry, Mr Goodrich.

Verity: Hey, I like your eyes.

Mrs Lips: [*Out of vision*] Trying to connect you. You are, probably, connected.

Graham goes on upstairs, where another phone is ringing.

◄ Reception, Ellfinn Publicity

*Mrs Lips, in her later thirties, wears a smart office jumpsuit, with group badges pinned to it. She sits behind a modern desk in a room with modern low chairs, Danish coffee tables; it is all slightly seedy, like a lesser 'Star Trek' set. **Mrs Lips** has a well-made up face and a confident modern style which substitutes for her lack of efficiency.*

Mrs Lips: Hello, Ellfinn, tops in design, he's on the phone to Mr Goodrich, can you hold, well, don't then.

Graham comes up to her desk, which has a sign saying: Reception: Mrs A Lipshultz.

Graham: This is Ellfinn Publicity?

Mrs Lips: You're the boy with the blocks from the printers.

Another of the several phones rings.

Mrs Lips: [*On the phone*] Hello, Ellfinn, best in, hello, lover, wasn't it good last night. I love those swinging places where they set fire to the food right at the table. Your best suit, was it really? [*To* **Graham**] Put them on the desk.

Graham: I'm not the boy with . . .

Mrs Lips: [*On the phone*] Isn't she on the Pill? [*A buzzer buzzes*] Oh, there's Mr Ellis on the other, can you hold? [*Puts down phone 1, picks up phone 2*] Hello, Mr

Ellis, no, he's on the other line about the Muesli . . .
[*Amused*] No, the blue ones today. I might and I
might not. Mr Ellis, I've got someone holding, can
you hold? [*Puts down phone 2, picks up phone 1*] Hello,
lover, oh damn. [*Puts down phone 1, picks up phone 2*]
Hello, Mr Ellis, oh sod. [*All phones down*] You're the
boy with the blocks from the printer.

Graham: No, I'm not. I have an appointment, with a
Mr Finn, about a . . .

Mrs Lips: [*Looking at a wallclock, saying 9.20*] Mr Finn
has no appointments till ten.

Graham: Yes, that's me. I'm early. I didn't want to be
late.

Mrs Lips: [*Amused*] Oh, you're Mr Peach.

Graham: That's right. Mr Peach.

Mrs Lips: Well, Mr Peach, I'm sorry, but he's on the
phone now, talking to Mr Goodrich about the . . .

Graham: Muesli promotion. Can I wait, please?

Mrs Lips: Take a seat, lover.

Graham *sits down and picks up* Studio: *A picture of a large
nude.* **Graham** *looks around.* **Mrs Lips** *is leaning on her elbow
at the desk, staring at him.*

Mrs Lips: You're ridiculously young, aren't you?

Graham: No. Not very.

Mrs Lips: Seventeen? Eighteen?

Graham: Nineteen.

Mrs Lips: Had it off yet?

Graham: Had what off?

Mrs Lips: It.

Graham: Oh. No.

Mrs Lips: Got a girlfriend?

Graham: Yes, I have.

Mrs Lips: I expect you give her a good run for her
money. What are you doing here?

Graham: I think there's a vacancy.

Mrs Lips: Henry's job? They're in a real mess without
  Henry.

Graham: Oh, yes. Did he leave?

Mrs Lips: I don't think so. He always meant to.
  Wanted to go to New York for the big time, make
  porno movies, that was one idea. But I don't think
  he left exactly. [*Phone*] Hello, Ellfinn, biggest
  and best, no, I think you've got the wrong
  number, we're not the blind. [*Phone down*] No,
  I think you'll find him in hospital with his legs
  in the air.

Graham: He had an accident?

Mrs Lips: I could tell you some stories about Henry.
  Oh, Mr Finn's off the line, maybe he'll see you now.
  [*Phone*] Oh, Mr Finn, that young, about the temporary, is it Henry's? . . . He came early so he
  wouldn't be late . . . Oh, okay, Mr Finn, fine,
  sending him through to you, Mr Finn. [*To* **Graham**]
  Kindly go through, Mr Peach. The door there
  marked 'Accounts Executive'.

Graham: Thank you.

Mrs Lips: [*As he goes*] Nervous, lover? Stay cool.
  Remember, under their suits they've all got dirty
  underwear, like you.

5 Finn's office, Ellfinn Publicity: Graham gets a job

Teddy Finn, *around thirty-five, is the complete executive, even
to office sunlamp. He has a sharp sixties shirt and tie, and a
Scandinavian office desk. On the walls, beside planning charts, are
modern reproductions: Warhol, Lichtenstein, Allen Jones.*

Finn: Hello, old boy, come in.

Graham: I'm sorry I'm early, I . . .

Finn: All right, old son, what's the good of a busy
  schedule if it can't be rearranged. Have a pew, like
  some coffee, muck out of a machine, I'm afraid, it's

the machine age. [*Picking up the phone*] Two coffees, Lipsy, how do you take it?

Graham: With cream and sugar, thank you.

Finn: [*Phone*] One black, one with two squirts. [*Phone down*] You fancy advertising?

Graham: Yes, I'm good at art, and my art-master . . .

Finn: Roger, right? Roger and I are both big in Rotary. Puff the weed?

Graham: No, thanks. Yes, Mr Martin thought I should try it before I went to university, to see my career potential.

Finn: Graham, forgive me if I speak like a bit of a Dutch uncle. But there's art, you know, what Rog teaches you, and then art, what we do here. This is commercial, a business, a hustle, what's it about, style turned into money. Because why, Graham? Because what people want now is style. A face to the world. You, you're a person. But you're competing with Polo mints. You've got to have style.

Graham: Yes. Right.

Finn: Look at me. Five years ago I was going round shops in a white Cortina, a commercial traveller, selling. I'd go in, little briefcase, and I'd ask to see the person who mattered. Mattered? They didn't matter. I realized what I've just told you. People want style. Style is publicity. I sold the boat, I took out no more than five hundred a year for four years. Look out there at the back now, Graham. See it?

Graham: The car?

Finn: Bentley. With a drinks cabinet. I sit in there and think about that Cortina. I say to myself, you've got almost too much. But this is a time of success stories. But success is there, Graham. I saw it, because I knew how to lay myself out. Bless you, Lipsy.

Mrs Lips: [*With coffee*] You're milk and sugar.

Finn: I was just saying. Advertising is laying yourself
out.

Mrs Lips: There's a lot of that round here.

Finn: Is Arthur there, Lipsy? My partner, the art
director. You might ask him to pop in.

Mrs Lips: I'll send him through, Mr Finn.

Finn: [*Staring after her as she goes*] She'll never understand a telephone, but look at that shape. Now then,
Graham . . .

Graham: Is there a job?

Finn: Right, well, let me level with you about that.
One of our artists has gone missing for a bit,
Graham. We hope he'll come back, we're not
replacing him permanently, but we need a fill in. So
I said to Rog at Rotary, know anyone, Rog. So you
come to be here. It's more oddjobbing than art-
work, Graham, is that understood? But if you like
us and we like ye. That's your work? Put it out on
the desk.

Graham: [*Opening his portfolio*] I wasn't sure what to
bring. I thought you might like to see the drawings I
do on weekends.

Finn: Oh, yes. [*He picks one up*] What's this?

Graham: My aunt. She's a real character.

Finn: Is she? What's this?

Graham: I'm glad you spotted that. I've been trying
to move towards abstract expressionism.

Finn: Ah.

Arthur Ellis *comes in. He is about* **Finn**'s *age, but is art to*
Finn's *commerce. He is Australian, wears a colourful shirt
unbuttoned to show his chest and a white suit.*

Ellis: I just took a few seconds out, Teddy, it's a kind
of steamy meeting in there.

Finn: This is Graham Peach. The boy Rog sent.

Ellis: Hi, Gram. Is this his work?

Graham: That's right.

Ellis: [*Looking through the portfolio quickly*] Hell, what is it?

Graham: Some sketches I made over the last year.

Finn: He's feeling his way towards an abstract expressionist style.

Ellis: I've been feeling for years, but I get more fun out of it than this.

Heather *in the doorway.* **Heather**, *the copywriter, has the look of a modern executive woman, glasses and Gucci.*

Heather: Arthur, can I disturb you a moment?

Ellis: You disturb me all the time, Heather. But I'm rather busy right now, I'll come and put my arm round your pretty shoulders in a minute.

Heather: Okay, but it's important.

Ellis: God, she looks like a panda in those glasses. What do you know about abstract expressionism? How many kinds of lettering do you know? Any posterwork or lettering? Done any photography? Ever made a film?

Graham: No.

Finn: We just want someone to stand in for Henry for a bit.

Ellis: Henry's a leading trained artist. This is a schoolboy.

Finn: I thought he could relieve the pressure. Try a bit of layout, fetch blocks from the printer, he knows we're only paying a few bob.

Ellis: Gram, up on that wall. What are they?

Graham: Lichtenstein. Warhol.

Ellis: All right. What, if anything, have they got?

Graham: A strong colour code. A sort of pop art style.

Ellis: You say that like you despise it. Now, I'll tell you what they've got. Seduction. Art is seduction,

seduction is art, right. Now your stuff over there, I look at it and I don't move. You know what I think, Gram? I think you're suburban. Like pop music?

Graham: A little.

Ellis: Jesus, Gram, either do or don't.

Finn: Have something to sell.

Graham: [*Folding up his portfolio*] I'm sorry. That's my best.

Ellis: Oh, come on, kid. Still want to try it?

Graham: What?

Ellis: Standing in for Henry. Of course it will only be a few odd jobs. We can't pay much.

Finn: We all have to start at the bottom. What do we say, Arthur, a tenner a week?

Ellis: Plus two more if he gets out of that bloody blazer. We'll take the chance, Gram. Come on, I'll show you the studio.

6 The public house

*Blurred and out of focus, we see **Henry** on the table. Loud music. Hands reaching up to him. **Henry** looks around, then jumps down to **Mrs Lips**.*

Over this we hear:

Ellis: Oh, Mrs Lips, here's Gram, he's going to work here.

Mrs Lips: Welcome, Graham. Trying to connect you . . .

Ellis: Come and meet Heather. She's our copywriter.

7 Heather's office, Ellfinn Publicity

Heather *is working at her desk in an efficient, orderly and quiet atmosphere.* **Ellis** *comes in with* **Graham**.

Heather: Hello, Arthur.

Ellis: Fine, how's Muesli.

Heather: You'll see, Friday morning. Who's this?

Ellis: Meet Gram. He's standing in for Henry.

Heather: Gram as in tele?

Graham: I'm Graham, actually.

Ellis: Come on, Gram, we'll put you to work.

8 The art studio, Ellfinn Publicity: Graham starts work

There are four drawing boards in the studio. At two, face to face, by the window, sit **Bruno**, *who is Polish, with an accent, and* **Martin**. *Then another board where* **Verity** *sits. The fourth, empty, must be* **Henry**'s.

Ellis: [*Coming in with* **Graham**] Hi there, people. I want to introduce Gram, he's coming to work here. There's Bruno, there's Martin, there's Verity. Gram's taking over Henry's board for a bit.

Verity: You're giving him Henry's job? Oh, you're kidding.

Ellis: Not Henry's job, Verity. He's just going to help out here. He's new to the game, so let him in easily. What happened to the Lee Furniture ad? A whale of a sale? Can he try that?

Martin: He certainly can for me.

Ellis: They'll set you up. They're a good crowd.

Martin: We're a great crowd.

Bruno: You may be a great crowd. I'm a lousy crowd.

Ellis: Okay, here's your board, there you sit. Looking at Verity.

Verity: Oh. You again. Arthur, he's a kid.

Ellis: He'll just work here till Henry comes out of hospital.

Martin: Oh, that's where Henry is. Henry's in hospital.

Verity: Henry isn't in hospital.

Ellis: He writes to us from hospital.

Verity: Henry's a master of deceit. Henry has addresses everywhere.

Ellis: Right, well, Gram, I leave you to it. Come by if you have difficulties, okay?

Ellis *goes.* **Graham** *sits at the board, wondering what to do.* **Verity** *is watching him.*

Verity: Hey, I like your nose.
Martin: I like it too.
Bruno: I like it too.

Graham *looks through the art on the desk: various cartoons and vaguely obscene drawings.*

Graham: What do I do?
Bruno: Where do you live, Graham?
Verity: And why?
Graham: Mapperley.
Bruno: Where the ladies go around their rose gardens with the little trowels. They say the sun shines there as it shines nowhere else.
Martin: They say the women are dusky and beautiful, and all the men are studs.
Graham: It's dull. I'm leaving it.
Bruno: Perhaps you are an angry young man. I had thought you were a little bit bourgeois.
Graham: I don't think so.
Bruno: Perhaps you pretend with us. You know we are boulevardiers, flaneurs, free spirits. No need to pretend. We understand the bourgeoisie. My mother was a bourgeois in drag.
Verity: You're straight from school, aren't you?
Martin: Many famous artists went to school.
Graham: I've left school. I'm waiting to go to university.
Bruno: Oh, the university. And for what subject? Wait, I know, you want to be a great scientist. Do you know Heisenberg?
Graham: I don't think so.

Martin: He's uncertain. Are you a dyke, Gram?

Bruno: How can he be a dyke. I expect he's an Oddfellow. Teddy Finn is an Oddfellow.

Graham: I'm not an Oddfellow.

Bruno: No, you're in Rotary. That is where you met Teddy Finn. Teddy Finn is very big in Rotary. Very little when he goes in a straight line, but very big in Rotary.

Graham: This advertisement. What do I do with it?

Martin: Take the rough and do a layout in Indian ink. Just sketch the lettering, they'll set that in type.

Verity: You don't understand, do you?

Graham: Yes. No.

Verity: You've never been to art school, have you?

Bruno: Henry went to art school. The bit of it that burned down.

Verity: God, look at you. You think you can draw because you won a prize in a children's art competition.

Bruno: Your nose is cold.

Martin: You suffer from chilblains.

Verity: And you come here trying to do Henry's job. Do you know who Henry is? Just the best commercial artist I've ever met.

Martin: A king among men.

Bruno: A giant among pygmies.

Verity: Henry was something else.

Martin: Other than what he was.

Bruno: [*Suddenly throwing open the window*] Hey, the girls, the dollies from the art school.

Verity: Oh, Christ.

Bruno: [*Shouting through the window*] Hey, how are you? You are some very pretty girls.

Verity: Henry's game.

Bruno: [*Through the window*] Listen, we're artists, fine talented people, with no girls. We haven't had a woman in five months. Want to come to the Lime Tree?

Martin: What for, she says.

Bruno: [*Through the window*] For a drink and some bad talk.

Martin: How many, she says. Coming, Gram?

Graham: Yes, fine.

Bruno: [*Through the window*] Three of us, three of you. Remember, kid, we're artists and we're hot stuff. [*Pulls the window down*]

Martin: Splendid.

Verity: Childish.

Bruno: Been in a pub, Gram?

Graham: Yes.

Bruno: Marvellous. I'm foreign, you can show me how to buy a round.

Martin: [*Coming over to Graham*] Okay, Graham. Let's show you what to do. You get some card from here and cut it first . . .

Verity: Right. Teach him from the beginning. I'm going to get some paper.

Bruno: [*As she gets to the door*] Don't let it worry you, Gram. Verity was Henry's girl friend. Everyone's really, little tramp.

Verity: [*Stopping in the doorway*] Did you call me a little tramp?

Bruno: I just asked Graham for a stamp.

Verity: [*To* **Graham**] Did he call me a little tramp?

Graham: I don't think so, no.

Verity: I'm a very big and famous tramp. [*She goes*]

Bruno: Also pissed at eleven in the morning.

Martin: As my landlady says: if God had intended us to drink, he'd have given us wings. Right, here's your rough, here's the card, here's the pen, here's a brush. Now, Graham, copy it. Okay?

Graham: [*Beginning to work*] Okay.

Martin: Fantastic. Another Henry.

9 The public house: Graham goes to the pub
Graham, Martin and **Bruno** are at a table. In front of them are sandwiches on a plate, and half drunk pints of beer.

Bruno: Well, what do you know, they didn't come. What is the matter with girls today? They make these promises, they don't keep them.

Martin: They'd have come for Henry. They always came for Henry.

Bruno: Hey, Gram, you're a nice young guy. How do you like it here? What do you think?

Graham: I hardly know yet.

Martin: You know, Henry was a master of the non-verbal seduction. This is the sexual act performed without discourse. Many have called it a great improvement. I've seen Henry stand there, against that bar, by the sign forbidding spitting, face forward, knees a little bent, no expression, none at all. The door opens, a girl comes in. She's well dressed, in green, it was, I think, little hat on top, as if to say: I am exact, I am perfected.

Bruno: Brown boots?

Martin: No, that was another time. Henry doesn't move, doesn't twitch. One would think thoughts of some great enterprise – building the Himalayas, climbing the North Pole – were in his head. The girl goes to the bar, pudically, and asks for a drink of a respectable kind, for an obviously respectable girl. Gin and tonic, or pomade, something that goes up your nose. She had a fine nose, like you, Gram. Henry is quite still. The girl is about to sit down, alone, when it is as if something draws her: a magnetism, a force. She veers towards Henry like a dowser with a twig. He puts her drink down on to the counter, untouched. He takes her hand, they go outside. Subsequent investigation reveals she has a car out there, a sports car. They put the top up, they get in. And no word is spoken, Gram, not one single word. And no word from me, Gram, about what happens in that car, except to say that fundamental parts are undoubtedly exchanged.

Bruno: Or so Henry says.

Martin: I sit here, supping brew. Ten minutes pass, then they come back. That little hat is tilted. The blue dress . . .

Bruno: The green dress.

Martin: The green dress is a touch disarrayed. Henry's expression is unchanged. The drink is still on the counter. Henry, ever the stylist, hands it to her. There is a sultry look in her eye, as if to say, the earth has moved for me, or at least the shock absorbers. She lifts the glass, to Henry. But Henry has resumed his position, looking forward, knees a little bent. He doesn't even look at that dewy pristine face, glass raised in salutation. Only now does he speak: 'Guinness,' he says. He always follows through with a Guinness. The girl goes white. She puts down her glass and goes. He never sees her again. As Samuel Beckett once observed, to my landlady actually, this is the age of the art of silence, and that goes for fornication too. Another half?

Graham: What happened to Henry?

Bruno: Ah, what did happen to Henry? They say he had an accident. He had a lot of those. With a life like Henry's, there are always accidents.

Martin: Henry had a motorbike. He needed it, for the quick getaway. Henry was a master of the quick getaway. Some called him a hero of sex. Some called him a male chauvinist pig. But he had every girl in the studio, have you done that, Bruno?

Bruno: No. They just bring me paper clips.

Graham: So he's in hospital?

Martin: Some say he's in hospital. Some say he's in a villa with a principessa in the Campagna. There were always something a little elusive about Henry. Gnomic. Henry always meant to leave us, you see.

Bruno: Henry was made for the big time. He had all the gifts. A great pop musician. His pornographic drawing was extraordinary. A little provincial city like this, where they hold the dances in the crematorium, that was too little for Henry. So maybe he took off. I think he took off.

Martin: Of course the only one who knows is Verity. They fought all the time, and they had everybody else, but they were serious, Henry and Verity. That's why you make her mad, sitting there in his place. Another half?

Graham: [*A decision*] No, look, I think I'll get back. I want to try and finish that ad.

Bruno: It's your lunch hour, Gram. Relax, there'll be nobody there.

Graham: [*Getting up*] I know, I want to try by myself. Anyway, if I have another, I won't be able to . . .

Bruno: To perform, Gram. Your performance will be impaired.

Graham: Yes.

Bruno: In this modern world you've got to perform. Did Teddy tell you that?

Graham: Yes.

Bruno: Teddy is predictable.

Martin: Henry, of course, performed. Some say that performance and Henry went together. I don't think there was anything he didn't perform. Any performance he didn't do.

Bruno: You remember the way back? Your orientations are normal?

Graham: Yes, thanks.
Martin: Come tomorrow.
Graham: Okay. Good.

10 Reception, Ellfinn Publicity: Graham works at lunchtime

Graham *comes in. The telephone rings as he goes through. He pauses, then picks it up.*

Graham: [*On the phone*] Hello, Ellfinn Publicity, the greatest in design . . . No, I'm sorry, I can't help you really. It's lunchtime and there's no one here.

He puts the phone down. He goes toward the studio. The other phone rings but he goes on to:

11 The art studio, Ellfinn Publicity: Graham talks to Verity

Graham *comes into the studio. He looks around: it is empty. He goes to his board: he finds the file of* **Henry***'s work. We see various items. They are signed Henry Feldman. Then* **Graham** *finds the nude drawing of* **Verity***. He stops. He pulls down the overhead light on his desk for a better view.*

Verity: [*In the doorway*] I like your ears.
Graham: [*Startled*] Oh. Hello. I didn't think anyone was here.
Verity: I'm here. I'm often here at lunchtime. I'm on a green salad diet. I don't really need to eat lunch. You knew that.
Graham: No, I didn't.
Verity: [*Coming into the room*] You do now. What are you doing? I thought you were picking up girls in the pub.
Graham: There weren't any.
Verity: Didn't they come? That's terrible. You were disappointed.
Graham: I didn't mind.

Verity: What do you know about girls?

Graham: Not much. I'd like to find out.

Verity: Would you? Why?

Graham: Well, obviously. Because I'm curious. Men are.

Verity: And you're a man. [*Seeing the drawing of herself out on the desk*] What are you doing with that? Why are you touching that?

Graham: I wanted to look at it.

Verity: I see. No girls at the pub, so you came back here to turn yourself on.

Graham: No. You all keep talking to me about Henry. So I wanted to see what was so fantastic about his work.

Verity: And do you see?

Graham: No. It's good. But it's not fantastic. It's not fantastic at all.

A pause.

Verity: What do you know about it? You're not even trained. Do you know why I don't like you?

Graham: Yes. I'm not Henry. And I'm sitting at his desk.

Verity: No. Henry is replaceable. But not by you. You see, you're not an artist, you're a spectator. I'm sure you've got it all planned out. You'll go off to university, you'll get a nice little second-class degree in psycho-socio-economics or something, then a nice little job in management. And you'll make a nice little second-class marriage to a nice little second-class wife and have nice little second-class sex in a nice little second-class suburb. Then you'll draw. That's how you'll use art. You'll feel terribly creative. Maybe you'll have little affairs, these are permissive times, even in the suburbs. But art will be your real adultery. Your

152

nasty little secret. And you'll think you're a Henry.

Graham: I don't even know Henry. I haven't met him.

Verity: I met him at art school. He must have been just your age. But not like you. You're clean, he was dirty. You're nice, nobody could say nice about Henry. He put his hand in my dress at the New Year Ball. Not a thing I generally permit. But Henry had the capacity to excite. Do you have the capacity to excite?

Graham: Obviously I don't.

Verity: I went outside and had it with him. Not a thing I generally permit. My first time. Well, I exaggerate, but nearly.

The telephone outside begins to ring again.

Graham: I see. Does that make his drawings good?

Verity: You know what Henry told me? Art and innocence don't mix. Art is a cheat, art is the art of marvellous cheating. You're so bloody innocent, Henry was a cheat. He certainly cheated me.

Graham: He cheated you? How?

Outside, the telephone stops, and we hear:

Mrs Lips: Hello, Ellfinn Publicity, best in design, can I help you?

Verity: Ellfinn Publicity, wonderful at everything, are you holding? Who are you holding? What are you holding? How would you like to hold me? Graham?

Graham: Me?

Verity: Come here, Graham.

Graham *gets up slowly.*

Verity: Come near. Offer to be Henry. Put your hand inside my dress.

Graham: No. Why? You don't like me.

Verity: It's what you wanted. Give me your hand. Everyone must learn the simple things. Now it goes right inside my dress. Close it, feel. Doesn't it give you a thrill? It gives everyone else a thrill.

Graham: No.

Verity: No? Why?

Graham: Mrs Lips is outside.

Mrs Lips: [*In the doorway*] There are some blocks to collect from the printer, Graham. When you're free.

Verity: [*Keeping **Graham**'s hand in her dress*] He's not free. There's no soap in the loo, Mrs Lips. Can there be soap in the loo?

Mrs Lips: If your ladyship says so. Come and see me, Graham, and I'll tell you the right way to get there.

Mrs Lips *goes*.

Verity: All right, get off me, Graham. Art must go on. There are some blocks to get from the printers.

Graham: Why did you do that?

Verity: It's a little lesson, Graham. You know, Graham, if you want it, it's easy to get. These are permissive times. They all give it away. Mrs Lips. Nice little Heather. You try them. Do try them. But don't try me. I am not of that order. What I like I request. And don't think it's that. Now Henry, Henry knew what I wanted. Maybe you'll find out.

Graham: I'm going.

Verity: Yes, you do. And Graham, try Mrs Lips. You do, Graham. How about a drink with me tomorrow? Shall we drink together, Graham?

Graham: I don't think so.

Verity: Well, don't worry, Graham. The others love you. You try them.

12 The passage and reception, Ellfinn Publicity

As **Graham** *comes out of the studio,* **Heather** *passes him, back from lunch.*

Heather: Hello, Henry, what have you been up to?
Graham: Graham, actually.
Heather: Right. Graham.

She moves on to **Mrs Lips***, at the desk.*

Mrs Lips: [*On phone*] Putting you through. [*To* **Graham**] Hey, Graham, you're a naughty boy. You be careful. That is one very troubled lady.
Graham: I have to get some blocks from the printer?
Mrs Lips: Their boy's off sick, here's a map, Longshore Printers in West Road. Say you're Ellfinn Publicity, ask for Mr Lee. You know, I'd stay away from that one. Remember what happened to Henry. Feel like seeing a film tonight?
Graham: Tonight? Well . . .
Mrs Lips: Okay, I don't ask twice. Next time you ask me. Take a number sixty-eight.

Graham *turns to go and encounters, in the doorway,* **Teddy Finn***, not too stable after a heavy lunch.*

Finn: Oh, Graham. Nothing like business lunches for stopping you doing business for the rest of the day. Well, what do you think? How do you like the great, bright, shiny wonderful world of advertising.
Graham: Very interesting, Mr Finn. A real hustle.
Finn: [*To* **Mrs Lips**] You know, that kid's learning.

13 The public house

Blurred camera, music, dancing in the bar. It is evening. We see **Henry** *and* **Mrs Lips***, kissing by a pillar.*

  Verity *is standing close by, looking satisfied.*
  Over this we hear the voice of **Ellis***:*

Ellis: Morning, Gram, you look smart. I thought maybe now you've been around a few days you'd like to join one of our promotion meetings. See how it's done.

14 Ellfinn Publicity: Graham conceives an ad
The artists are gathering in reception ready for the meeting.

Graham: Yes, thanks, Mr Ellis, I would.

Finn: [*Opening his door*] Sorry to keep you, I had *Harper's Bazaar* on the line. Graham, how goes it?

Graham: All very interesting, Mr Finn.

Ellis: Great, here's Heather. Your day today.

Heather: Oh, I hope they like it.

Mrs Lips: Coffee orders, Graham.

Graham: Black one, please, Mrs Lips.

Ellis: Where's Verity? I'd sort of like to get started, Teddy. I've got an executive lunch today.

Martin: My landlady read in *The Sunday Times* yesterday that scampi causes piles.

Finn: I've not seen her, Arthur.

Ellis: You're kidding, Martin, is he kidding?

Bruno: Steak Diane causes acne.

Martin: Boeuf Stroganoff has been linked with epilepsy.

Bruno: Veal à la Marsala blocks the menstrual flow.

Ellis: Thank God you're kidding.

Martin: Who's kidding? Why do executives die in their forties?

Ellis: I think we'll start, Verity or no Verity. Now, just to explain to our innocent bystander, Gram. Today we're trying to round up a coherent package for our Muesli promotion. Muesli's a kind of breakfast cereal they eat a lot of in Switzerland, Gram. It's got a healthy association, like cow dung. It's kind of expensive, and we're trying for a sound market profile for this new to Britain product, right.

Finn: The point is to go in at the right angle.

Ellis: Now Heather with my advice has been rounding out this package and we're here to see if it zings. Right, Heather.

Verity *comes in, wearing dark glasses.*

Finn: You're late.

Ellis: Come on, Verity, sit down.

Heather: Okay, up to now this has been a specialist health food store sort of product. Now we aim to bring it into the mass market. Arthur, should I start with the storyboard for the television commercial?

Ellis: Right, Heather, but let's just state, this is a big thing for Ellfinn. A first, the first tele commercial in the studio. Okay, Heather.

Heather: Right, well, something like this. Int. Studio, suburban bedroom, early morning. A nice bed with a nice young couple in it.

Verity: How did you research this, Heather?

Ellis: Attractive but faithful. We don't say they're married, we don't say they're not.

Verity: [*Whispering to* **Graham**] Did you try Mrs Lips?

Graham: No.

Heather: He wears pyjamas, say blue, she has a long nightdress on, white. Grey studio light through the windows, washed out colour, the Wim Wenders look. Then jingle over, a really contemporary close harmony group. Now, during this, okay, the light changes, the room turning from grey to yellow, like the sun's broken in.

Verity: Okay.

Heather: Right, the jingle, it goes:
What makes the dawn glow?
What makes the corn grow?

What makes the sun shine?
What makes the nuts fine?

Verity: What makes the nuts fine?

Ellis: Can it, Verity, this stuff has corn and nuts in it, we have to establish them. Then what, Heather?

Heather: Then a deep voice narrator over says: Raisins and sultanas too.

Verity: Because they're hard to find rhymes for.

Heather: Cut to breakfast table in sunlight. The couple eat Muesli, show the pack. The deep voice narrator says out of vision: What gets you up in the morning? And the man turns full face to camera and says: Muesli, uesli. Deep voice narrator: The day starts with a shine when you start with Muesli. What gets *you* up in the morning? And the girl turns to the camera, smiles, and says . . .

Verity: Muesli uesli.

Heather: Right.

Mrs Lips: I think it's terrific, Heather.

Graham *has been looking round the table: shots of the faces of* **Heather**, **Verity**, **Mrs Lips**. *We hear an echo from an earlier scene:*

Martin: [*Out of vision*] Some called him a hero of sex. Some called him a male chauvinist pig. But he had every girl in the studio, have you ever done that, Bruno?

Ellis: Right, I'd just like to get our relatively innocent observer in on this. What did you think, Gram? Did it hit you at all?

Graham: Me? Oh. You say it's Swiss?

Ellis: It's what the Swiss eat, right, Gram.

Graham: Yes, well, I wonder whether we could be less domestic and use the Swiss angle. A steamer on Lake Lucerne, cows with cattle bells in a field, and in the background those funny little green hills in

Appenzell. Then maybe a train coming out of the Gotthard, breakfast being served in the dining car, a smart attendant serving a cosmopolitan couple, and what are they having?

Verity: Muesli uesli.

Ellis: I see, Gram. You mean, we're offering immediate deep pleasure, not just dry mush with raisins, right?

Finn: You'd take it further upmarket, towards the ABs?

Graham: Yes. That's what I mean.

Heather: [*Tears in her eyes*] But you said move it downmarket, into the suburbs.

Ellis: Right, but you see what Gram's saying, in his simple way. He's saying we're concerned with poetry, we argue by metaphor, we paint with images, right, Gram?

Graham: Right.

Ellis: He's saying we're not just selling goods, we're selling fine experiences, utopia. He's explaining that most human lives are impoverished. And our aim is to enrich them.

Verity: Especially if they're ours.

Ellis: Okay, can it, Verity. I know you think I'm some antipodean fart, some bloody marsupial stuffing banknotes into my pouch. But believe me, I'm a hypocrite with genuine convictions, and I go with Gram. I like that Gotthard, bursting out into the light. The cow is shit I can lose.

Heather, *in tears, folds up her briefcase and hurries out.*

Ellis: Oh, Jesus. Look, let's take a break. Someone go after her.

Verity: Go after her, Graham.

Graham *gets up to go.*

Verity: [*Quietly, grabbing his arm*] I think you've got something after all, kid.

15 The public house
Blurred camera, music, dancing in the bar. It is evening. **Heather** *is standing by a pillar, laughing.* **Henry** *comes over and kisses her.*

Over this we hear **Martin**'s *voice, saying:*

Martin: What makes the sun shine? What makes the nuts fine? What makes your nuts fine, Bruno?

Bruno: [*Also out of vision*] Muesli, uesli.

16 The bar of the public house
It is the same bar in different mood: lunchtime. **Martin**, **Bruno** *and* **Graham** *are sitting over sandwiches and beer.*

Graham: I should have kept quiet.

Bruno: Gram is very upset about Heather being very upset. Gram is very sensitive.

Martin: Oh, come on, Gram, you were good. Guess who would have been proud of you if he'd been here?

Bruno: Alfred Lord Tennyson.

Martin: Henry. Did you see those tears come?

Graham: Did I do that? I just wanted to show I could have an idea. I wasn't even listening properly.

Martin: But what an idea, Graham. Breakfast on the Gotthard. What a mind.

Bruno: Why was Verity in shades?

Martin: The glasses? I think, I think Verity spent last night up there on the tiles. With you, Graham.

Graham: No, not with me.

Bruno: You're a great team, you and Verity. A truly Henry morning.

Graham: Must we always bring in Henry?

Martin: You might say he exercises an obsessive fascination. He lightened up the dull days.

Graham: How?

Martin: How to sum up the power and fascination of Henry in a phrase, Bruno?

Bruno: He was a bastard.

Martin: Right. He was a bastard, he smelled rather a lot, he was deep into porn, does that suggest his charm?

Graham: No.

Martin: Okay, to try again: Henry walked the knife-edge. And, as the noted existentialist Jean-Paul Sartre once said, at a dinner party given by my landlady actually, we must all walk the knife-edge. I thought you did a bit, this morning.

Bruno: Sartre said that.

Martin: I remember it well. My landlady attempted a rebuff. I rebuff you, Jean-Paul, she said, taking up a Hegelian position, with both legs crossed. Chère madame, said Sartre in his gracious way, truly you have reason. But, as I once proved conclusively, in a dining car on the Gotthard, existence precedes essence, and zis means we all walk ze knife-edge.

Graham: Okay, what did Henry do?

Bruno: Gram's growing suspicious about Henry.

Martin: You'd like an example. One day at art-school, a sense of vertiginous despair overtook him. He remarked on it: 'I'm overtook with a sense of vertiginous despair,' he told me. Van Gogh would have cut off an ear, but what Henry chose to do was to get up on the balcony, five floors up, and walk round it on his hands. A small expectant crowd gathered, shouting 'Come on, fall.' The fire engines came, they put out nets and held them, and girls stood on the grass below and flashed their thighs, trying to get him to jump. But Henry kept on, round and round the balcony, twenty or thirty times. Then he jumped, landed in the net, dusted

161

himself off, went into the gents to wash off, fell and broke his nose. I think it was five days in hospital that time. And zat is what at the Deux Magots we call walking ze knife-edge.

Bruno: You need a drink. My round.

Graham: Not for me, thanks. I'm going back.

Martin: [*As* **Graham** *goes*] Your devotion astounds. Give her my love.

17 Reception area and Heather's office at Ellfinn Publicity: Graham finds Heather unhappy

Graham *comes into the empty reception area, and walks towards the studio.*

There is a noise. He turns to see **Heather**'s *door open. She is opening and shutting filing cabinets, noisily and angrily.*

Graham: Heather, look, I'm sorry. Are you all right?

Heather: That bloody sod Ellis. I've been chasing him for weeks, asking him whether we're going up or down market. First he's up, then he's down, then he bloody goes up again.

Graham: He wants you to do it again?

Heather: He came in before lunch, put his bloody arm round my shoulders, said: 'Let me put my arm round your pretty shoulders, honey, that young boy spotted what we didn't. It didn't sedooce, Heather. My ears didn't jump up and down. I think we might even try the cow.'

Graham: I really didn't mean to . . .

Heather: Was it her idea or yours?

Graham: Who?

Heather: You know who, Verity.

Graham: It just happened, Heather. He asked me and I said the first thing that came into my head.

Heather: It just happened. Look, Jesus, get out of here, Henry.

Graham: I'm not Henry. I'm Graham. Gram.

Heather: [*Tears coming*] Oh, God, come in. Shut the door.

Graham *shuts the door.*

Graham: You thought I'd planned it with Verity? Why would I?

Heather: It's what she always did with Henry. A sort of game.

Graham: A game? Why?

Heather: Don't you understand about Henry? He was corrupt. He wanted to get inside everybody. People were a kind of . . . provocation to him. He had a lesson for them, be like him, go down in the dirt with him.

Graham: Why does everyone admire him, then?

Heather: We all need our lessons. We all have our weak spots. He thought I was stuffy, frigid, I had to be changed.

Graham: You're not.

Heather: Hell, what's the matter with me? I'm a professional, I've been in this game three years, I have a diploma. I ought to be able to take rejection.

Graham: Of course you can.

Heather: What do you know? You're a kid. I don't suppose you've ever been through rejection.

Graham: Yes I have. Often.

Heather: Help me take it, Graham. Cheer me up. Make me feel good. Will you?

Graham: Yes.

Heather: Is anyone out there?

Graham: No, they're all at lunch.

Heather: Press the button on the door. Come over here. [*She drops into her chair*] Come here, come down.

Graham: On top?

Heather: Kiss me.

They kiss. **Heather** *kisses his face avariciously.*

Heather: I'm not stuffy. Not frigid.
Graham: Did you do this with Henry?
Heather: I'm not, I'm not.

The telephone rings.

Heather: Who's that?
Graham: I don't know. Leave it.
Heather: Let me reach it. I expect it's Mrs Lips. She
has antennae like an ant. [*She picks up the phone*] Yes?
Yes, he's here. [*She hands the phone to* **Graham**]
Graham: Hello? Oh, Verity. No, I wasn't having a
drink with you. No. [*He puts the phone down*]
Heather: Find my glasses. Over there. By the filing
cabinet. You set this up too. You and her.
Graham: No.
Heather: How did she know you were here?
Graham: I don't know. She has lunch in the studio.
Heather: [*Putting on her glasses*] She told you to go down
on me.
Graham: Why would she?
Heather: It's the game, isn't it.
Graham: There's no game. I must go.
Heather: Okay.
Graham: Okay.
Heather: I do have a suggestion. Come to my flat
tonight, if you like. I have a nice little flat in the
park. I'll cook you a meal.
Graham: Is it a good idea?
Heather: I'm not frigid.
Graham: No.
Heather: I'll wait on the corner at six.
Graham: Yes.

Graham *opens the door. We see* **Mrs Lips** *sitting in reception,
talking on the phone.*

Mrs Lips: Oh, Graham, some blocks to take to the printers. How is she?

Graham: Who? Oh, Heather, fine.

Mrs Lips: She's a soft little thing, that one. You'd do better with me. I'm good company, Graham.

Graham: Where are the blocks for?

Mrs Lips: Here they are, I packed them, take them to the newspaper, ask for Mr Jackman. It's on Market Street.

Graham: I know, I've been there.

Mrs Lips: Well, you've been everywhere now, haven't you? Take me to a film tonight. There's a good one on at the Odeon.

Graham: I can't tonight . . .

Mrs Lips: Okay, I've told you, I don't ask twice.

Graham: But I could tomorrow.

Mrs Lips: You know, you were good this morning, Graham. Really good.

18 The public house

Blurred camera, music, night time. In a booth, **Henry** *is holding* **Mrs Lips** *and* **Heather**. **Verity** *comes over: a confrontation. Over this scene, we hear:*

Martin: How was it with Heather?

Bruno: How was it with Mrs Lips?

19 The studio, Ellfinn Publicity: Graham is ink-stained

The work routine of the studio: **Bruno**, **Martin**, **Verity** *and* **Graham** *are all at their boards.*

Martin: It's said that Mrs Lips has dyed her pubic hair blue. To show her allegiance to the Tory Party. Is it true, Graham?

Graham: No.

Bruno: Not blue?

Graham: She's a member of the Liberal Party.

Martin: My landlady's a Liberal. She wears two vests. Does Heather wear two vests?

Graham: No.

Bruno: Ah, doesn't she?

Graham: You can see through her see-through blouse.

Martin: Why so secretive, Graham?

Bruno: Henry told us everything.

Verity *stands up. She takes a bottle of Indian ink. She pours it over the advertisement* **Graham** *is working on, splashing his clothes.*

Graham: Christ!

Verity: [*Going out*] Just going to the loo.

Bruno: Well, she's changed. Now she really likes you, Graham.

Martin: We said she'd come round.

Bruno: She always did that with Henry. After he'd been tomcatting. Hey, the girls. [*Throwing up the window*] Hey girls, how are you, see you at the Lime Tree, three of us . . .

Martin: You do want to come, Graham? You're not too tired?

Graham: No. Fine.

20 The public house: Graham encounters Verity

It is evening. **Bruno** *carries a tray of drinks to the table where* **Graham** *and* **Martin** *sit. With them are* **three girls** *from the art college, youthful stylists in extreme dress.*

Girl 1: Who?

Martin: Henry.

Girl 1: Who's he?

Girl 2: Oh, Henry. Did he come in here a lot?

Girl 3: In leather with a bent nose?

Bruno: Leather was worn, the nose was asymmetrical, he did come in here.

Girl 1: No, I don't know him.

166

Girl 2: You do. Fair hair.

Girl 3: It wasn't fair. I never saw him in here. He went to that other pub.

Martin: Anyway he's gone. Graham's come instead.

Girl 1: This is you.

Bruno: This is him. The stud of Ellfinn Publicity. As Arthur Dolliver says of him: Gram, you look to me like a real sixties person.

Girl 2: A stud, are you?

Martin: Touch him. Feel the quality.

Graham: Martin, tell me something. Does Henry really exist?

Martin: Does Henry exist! Does this stone I'm kicking exist!

Girl 1: Does who exist?

Girl 2: The one we were talking about.

Bruno: Has anyone ever seriously questioned whether Henry existed before?

Martin: Not when he was here. Let's put the question the other way round. Why would he not exist?

Bruno: Gram thinks we made him up. To enrich our impoverished lives.

Graham: All right. Where is he?

Girl 3: I expect he's over the other pub.

Bruno: He went to America.

Girl 1: Isn't he the one who had some kind of accident? Just outside here, on his bike? After he had a row with that girl.

Girl 2: What girl?

Girl 1: The girl over there.

They turn to look. **Verity**, *in her dark glasses, is sitting at the bar. She beckons to* **Graham**.

Bruno: I told you she liked you. She only pours ink over the art of people she really cares about.

Graham *picks up his drink and walks toward her.*

Verity: Hello, it's Graham.

Graham: Why did you do that, Verity?

Verity: Oh, the ink? I thought you'd been neglecting me lately. I thought it was time we had a talk.

Graham: Have a drink.

Verity: Not here. I find your friends very infantile. I have a flat, Graham.

Graham: I don't think it's a good idea.

Verity: It's all right. Henry's gone. They're looking at us, let's go.

21 The public house

It is evening. Blurred camera, music. **Verity** *and* **Henry** *are having a quarrel.* **Henry** *turns.* **Verity** *hits him on the back. Over this, we hear* **Verity**'s *voice:*

Verity: Come on in, Graham. Here's my flat. This is my inner sanctum. What do you think?

Graham: [*Out of vision*] Very nice.

22 Verity's flat: Verity wants Graham

It is a top-floor flat in an old house, very under-furnished, with an old settee, some old chairs, and a floor-level mattress in the middle of the room. There is also a drawing board.

Verity: It's not nice at all. I don't own much, I like to move a lot. No New Dimension furniture, like Heather's. I don't cook lasagna, like Mrs Lips. Just my settee, my cooker. My board, my bed. It's enough, nobody comes here. You're favoured, Graham. It's not a thing I generally permit.

Graham *looks out of the window.*

Graham: It's a good view. You can see a lot of the city.

Verity: Oh now, you came for a drink. Let me get you one. I have plenty. No food, just my lettuce. But plenty of drink.

Graham *looks at the paintings and drawings that cover the walls.*
We see that all these heads and bodies are images of Verity.

Graham: Oh, beer, please.

Verity: Well, there's plenty to drink, but only one kind. I drink scotch. You'll think me a bad hostess. You're used to better.

Graham: No, scotch is fine.

Verity: I should have bought beer. I want to please you, Graham.

Graham: I thought you despised me.

Verity: Opinions change. You change. You did what I said, didn't you?

Graham: Did I?

Verity: You tried Heather, you tried Mrs Lips. What was it like, Graham? What was your pleasure like?

Graham: Is that what you wanted to talk about?

Verity: Didn't you do it to please me, Graham?

Graham: No. It was nothing to do with you at all.

Verity: You're mad because I don't have beer. I'll go downstairs and get some. I have generous neighbours.

Graham: I think I ought to go.

Verity: I can't let you go like that. I want you to look at the paintings. I want to hear what you think of them. You know who did them, don't you? You recognize the inimitable style?

Graham: Are they his?

Verity: This is where he worked. He lived here.

Graham: But he's gone.

Verity: Oh, he's gone all right. We shall not see him again.

Graham: He had an accident?

Verity: No, he went away. He flew from Heathrow with an open return. His destination was Rome. He carried with him two suitcases and a drawing

board. He wore a calf-length suede coat. His
passport was in his own name. It was an afternoon
flight. I said good-bye to him at the airport, and he
left me this.

Verity *removes her dark glasses, to show a badly bruised eye.*

Graham: He hit you?

Verity: That was his style. His style was influenced by
the Futurists. You've only to look round you. You
were going to tell me what you thought of them.

Graham: They're good.

Verity: But not so bloody fabulous. That's what you
said. As you remarked, times changes. Styles take a
nosedive. New tendencies come in. That's what I
thought when he left me at the airport. Off you go,
Henry. New tendencies will come in. Of course
when an intimate friend goes, then you feel empty.

Graham: Yes.

Verity: I asked myself, where could there be another
Henry. I knew one thing, it wasn't you. Innocent,
suburban. Unbutton my dress. It undoes down the
front.

Graham: Not again, Verity.

Verity: It's not like last time. Remember what I said?
When I wanted you I'd tell you?

Verity *unbuttons the dress herself: it falls to the floor.*

Verity: Am I nice? Do I look good?

Graham: Yes.

Verity: Come here, Graham. I do feel very empty.
Come near, reach out, don't touch. I want you to do
something special. Do it the way Henry did.

Graham: What?

Verity: Henry never touched me. He got all that from
the others. Heather, Mrs Lips, they all give it away.
That disgusts me.

Graham: You told me you and he . . .

Verity: I told you that, you believe things. He was never inside me ever. You know why we were here. You know what he did to me.

Graham: What?

Verity: He drew me. Draw me, Graham, I want to see your style.

Graham *goes slowly over to the drawing board.*

23 Verity's flat

Blurred camera. **Verity**'s *posing,* **Henry** *drawing. We see* **Henry**'s *face as he shouts something. Then he goes out of the room.* **Verity** *runs to the door to shout after him. There is the noise of a motorcycle starting, and then* **Verity**'s *voice is heard over this:*

Verity: Graham was good last night.

Bruno: [*Out of vision*] Please, I'm too young, I can't bear it.

24 The studio, Ellfinn Publicity: Graham and the morning after

The artists *all at work at their boards.*

Verity: I took him to my flat. I don't own much, I like to move a lot. You were good, Graham, weren't you?

Martin: My landlady had a vision last night. She explained it at breakfast. Comets fell from the sky. There was a sound as of celestial music. Four white horsemen appeared to her. I bet there was something going on somewhere, she said.

Verity: Don't underestimate Graham.

Martin: Right. Remember him six weeks ago. His hair stuck up. He wore a blazer. Look at him now.

Mrs Lips: [*Looking into the studio*] Graham. You're wanted. Mr Finn wants to see you.

Graham: Oh, thanks, Mrs Lips.

Martin: McCann Erickson want him.

Bruno: Lyndon Johnson needs his advice.

Verity: I want you tonight, Graham.

Martin: Fantastic.

Graham *goes out.*

25 Reception, Ellfinn Publicity

Graham, *coming along the corridor, passes Heather's door.*

Heather: Graham.

Graham: Hello.

Heather: You didn't come, Graham.

Graham: I couldn't last night. I had some work to do.

Heather: You could have picked up the phone.

Graham: Things are pretty busy.

Heather: Too busy for tonight?

Graham: Well, right.

Heather: You're quitting.

Graham: No, really. I'll see you in a couple of days, okay.

Heather: If you want to quit.

Graham: No, look, we're good together. Stay calm. I'll see you.

He kisses her head. Then he goes back out into the corridor, towards **Mrs Lips** *at the reception desk.*

Mrs Lips: [*On phone*] Hold on, Mr Goodrich, hold, hold, hold. Trying to connect you, trying to connect you. Failing. [*To* **Graham**] Hello, lover.

Graham: [*Nodding in the direction of* **Finn**'s *office*] What's it about?

Mrs Lips: I don't know. Come by on Friday? I've got these new records.

Graham: Look, I'm busy Friday. Are you in Sunday afternoon?

Mrs Lips: It's not my sabbath, it's your sabbath. Is it her?

Graham: Who?

Mrs Lips: That one. The one who did for Henry.

Graham: She's okay.

Graham *knocks on* **Finn**'s *door.*

Mrs Lips: Graham, she's crazy.

26 Finn's office: Graham reaches an ending

Graham *comes into the room.* **Finn** *and* **Ellis** *sit there.*

Ellis: Ah, Gram, come on in, take a pew.

Finn: That's right, sit down, Graham. Cup of coffee? How do you like it?

Graham: Oh, thanks. Black, please.

Finn: [*Picking up phone*] Lipsy, three black ones. And no calls.

Ellis: Well, Gram, how goes it?

Graham: Fine.

Ellis: You like the life.

Graham: It's great.

Ellis: Right, you look great. Okay, fine, well, that's what we wanted to talk about. You remember our deal, a temporary arrangement till Henry came back? How do you feel about that now?

Graham: Well, Arthur, I think I've really learned a lot here. I also think I'm good.

Finn: You have something to sell now, Graham.

Graham: I think my work's strong, things have come together, it's as good as anybody's here.

Ellis: I think that's right, Gram.

Graham: So I wondered, now Henry's gone, whether there's a way to make the situation permanent.

Ellis: What do you mean, Henry's gone?

Graham: He's in Rome, making films.

Ellis: Who told you that?

Graham: Verity.

Ellis: Look, Gram, Verity is a lying cow, if you'll pardon me. Henry's just got out of hospital. He's been there ever since his accident.

Graham: He didn't have an accident.

Ellis: He drove down the road at sixty on his motor-bike and went over the top of a car. I saw him yesterday, Gram.

Finn: We're sorry, Graham. I don't know why Verity lies to you. But you see what it means?

Graham: He's coming back.

Finn: He wants to start back in tomorrow. We'd like to keep you on but, and don't let this out of that door, we've not been doing too well lately.

Ellis: We lost the Muesli account, it's a cut-throat age. They wanted to go right down market. Henry has his crutty side, he's not like you, Gram, you're a good kid. But we really need him back.

Mrs Lips comes in with the coffee.

Finn: Oh, Mrs Lips, thanks. I was just telling Graham. Henry's coming back tomorrow.

Mrs Lips: Henry?

Ellis: That'll stir things up.

Mrs Lips: [*Handing round coffee*] What happens to Graham?

Ellis: Well, Gram was always temporary, Lipsy.

Mrs Lips: Well, I'm sorry. We'll miss you, Graham.

Mrs Lips goes.

Ellis: You know, Gram, that's right. We'll miss you. We've developed a real respect for you round here.

Finn: That's right.

Ellis: In fact we wanted to ask. If, in a few weeks, someone on our staff left, say Verity, would you . . .?

Graham: Well, thanks, but I don't think so. I think I ought to get my nice little second-class degree and find a nice little job in middle management somewhere.

Ellis: Okay, Gram. Well, it's been nice having you. As the actress said to the bishop.

Finn: That's right, Graham. Give my best to Rog.

Graham: Yes. Thanks.

Finn: *Ciao.*

27 A street in a provincial city

It is night. Blurred camera. A motorcycle comes at speed along the street. The rider is goggled and leathered.

An intersection: a car comes out. The bike hits it. A noise of splintering. The rider flies into the air.

Verity's voice is heard:

Verity: What are you doing? Leaving?

Graham: [*Also out of vision*] Right. Someone else is coming.

28 The studio, Ellfinn Publicity

Graham *is putting his drawings into his portfolio.*

Verity: You can't leave.

Graham *shakes hands with* **Bruno** *and* **Martin**.

Bruno: You know, Gram, they could try every drunk in the city, and they'd never get one better than you.

Verity: Who's coming?

Graham: Nobody I know.

29 Reception, Ellfinn Publicity

Graham *is walking out.* **Heather** *is standing in her doorway.*
Mrs Lips *is at her desk.*

Mrs Lips: Sorry, lover.

At the end of the corridor, **Verity** *looks after him.*

Graham *goes out of the door marked* **Ellfinn**, *which swings to hide her.*

30 The staircase, Ellfinn Publicity: Graham and Henry meet

Graham *comes out of the door and stands for a moment at the top of the stairs. He looks down. Someone is beginning to come up the stairs.*

Graham *begins to descend. They pass in the middle.* **Henry** *turns back to look down at* **Graham**, **Graham** *turns to look at* **Henry**. *The shot is frozen as the credits roll.*

The World Health Report 1995

Bridging the gaps

Report of the Director-General

World Health Organization
Geneva
1995

Reprinted 1995, 1996

WHO Library Cataloguing in Publication Data

World health report 1995: bridging the gaps
  1.World health 2.Health policy - trends
  3.Health status 4.World Health Organization

ISBN 92 4 156178 5 (NLM Classification: WA 540.1)

Information concerning this publication can be obtained from:
Office of World Health Reporting
World Health Organization
1211 Geneva 27, Switzerland.
Fax: (41-22) 791 4870

Design and layout by WHO Graphics
Printed in France
95/10375 – Sadag – 7500
95/10609 – Sadag – 4000
96/11104 – Sadag – 1000